THE SEDUCTIVE LOVE OF
A LADY

JANE LARK

Boldwood

First published in 2015. This edition published in Great Britain in 2025 by Boldwood Books Ltd.

Copyright © Jane Lark, 2015

Cover Design by Head Design Ltd.

Cover Images: Shutterstock and Head Design Ltd.

The moral right of Jane Lark to be identified as the author of this work has been asserted in accordance with the Copyright, Designs and Patents Act 1988.

Every effort has been made to obtain the necessary permissions with reference to copyright material, both illustrative and quoted. We apologise for any omissions in this respect and will be pleased to make the appropriate acknowledgements in any future edition.

A CIP catalogue record for this book is available from the British Library.

Paperback ISBN 978-1-83703-372-0

Large Print ISBN 978-1-83703-373-7

Hardback ISBN 978-1-83703-371-3

Ebook ISBN 978-1-83703-374-4

Kindle ISBN 978-1-83703-375-1

Audio CD ISBN 978-1-83703-366-9

MP3 CD ISBN 978-1-83703-367-6

Digital audio download ISBN 978-1-83703-370-6

This book is printed on certified sustainable paper. Boldwood Books is dedicated to putting sustainability at the heart of our business. For more information please visit https://www.boldwoodbooks.com/about-us/sustainability/

Boldwood Books Ltd, 23 Bowerdean Street, London, SW6 3TN

www.boldwoodbooks.com

1

Mary watched Andrew, her husband of one day. He stood before his mirror, tying his cravat. He had changed into evening clothes, as had she. 'I shall be only a moment more.' He watched his reflection as he tied the knot into a clever decoration and set it just so.

He had laced her corset and now she waited with her back turned so he would button up her dress.

He turned to her.

His fingers brushed against her bottom through her petticoats and worked their way up as he slotted each little ivory button into place.

They had spent a quiet afternoon over the chessboard.

It was easier to believe they could form some sort of an acceptable marriage from this mess when he behaved companionably.

She had pulled herself together after he left her alone to go riding this morning. Yes, he still claimed to love her. But a man is known by the company he keeps, and his friends were sly, scheming, cruel-minded men. Also, he had failed to mention that he had asked her sister-in-law to go to bed with him. How could she believe in his love when she knew those other things.

Yet, whether he loved her or not, he was now her husband. She made this choice, she had no option but to live with him, and therefore she must make their marriage work. After all, she still loved him, and sharing his bed was enjoyable.

'There you are, all done.'

Mary caught sight of her image in the mirror. She was unable to do anything elaborate with her hair other than to twist it into a tight chignon and pin it up. It looked acceptable.

She turned to the small bag in which she had put her personal items and jewellery. She searched out a pretty silver comb and looked in her mirror to position it in her hair, to make it look more ornamental. Then found out a necklace with a small silver cross which her father bought for her.

'Here, let me.' Andrew took it and looked at it for a moment before securing it about her neck.

The feeling of the new wedding ring on her finger called its presence, she had kept her finger curled a little all afternoon so it would not slip off. Then earlier Andrew had tied a thin band of leather about it to stop it slipping.

'Are you ready?' he asked.

'Yes, apart from my shawl.'

It was on the bed. He picked it up and lay it about her shoulders. At the same moment Mary heard a strong knock strike the front door downstairs.

'That will be my parents.'

'Perfect timing then.'

'Yes.' She turned to hurry away.

'Mary.' His fingers caught her forearm and stopped her. 'Let me walk you down. What time will you return?'

'Midnight, or possibly later. I am unsure.'

'Then I shall come home before midnight. I will be here when you return.'

She thought he liked her at least. She knew he liked her body, but she thought he liked her company too. A vast chasm stretched between like and love, though.

They walked down the stairs in silence.

A footman clothed in her half-brother's, the Duke of Pembroke, livery, waited at the open door. John and his wife, Kate, must have come with her parents. The footman stepped aside as Andrew's fingers gently closed around her upper arm and led her out.

Another footman held the carriage door open, waiting to help her. She saw her father and John inside the carriage. They watched Andrew with accusing eyes.

Andrew's fingers fell to hold her hand instead of her arm, so she could use his hand to steady herself as she climbed the step into the carriage.

'Goodbye. I hope you enjoy your evening,' he said.

She glanced back and saw a genuine look of goodwill.

He did like her. She was sure of that at least.

She smiled. 'Goodbye. Enjoy your evening too.'

He bowed his head.

She settled into the seat beside Kate. Then the carriage door shut. Andrew raised a hand as the carriage pulled away.

Mary rested back against the squabs, still looking through the window, unable to look at her family. The infancy of her marriage was nothing like theirs. It felt as if she were playing a game of husband and wife. She had stepped back into the life of her childhood this morning, when she walked back to John's town mansion to collect some books and sewing to keep her occupied if Andrew was not in his rooms, and now again, she was with her family, going to a musical evening, without her husband.

'Why is he not coming?' John asked.

'It is not Andrew's sort of entertainment.' This morning, she told them he was in a business meeting. If he continued to choose not to face her family, she would spend her marriage weaving a whole web of white lies to prevent them disliking him any more than they already did. She wanted her parents to think she was happy. If they were angry with Andrew, it would only make everything worse.

'What is his preferred entertainment?' her father asked.

He had not told her.

Kate's fingers touched her hand. 'It was good of him to walk you out. I am sure in future he may be persuaded to join us.'

'I hope not. I do not want him anywhere near you, Katherine,' John said.

'He is Mary's husband,' Kate answered.

'Kate is right, John,' Mary's mother agreed. 'We must make the best of this now for Mary's sake.'

'But I cannot stand him either,' her father responded.

Mary looked at them all. 'Please, do not argue... and must you keep glaring so horribly at him? I was silly to let him persuade me, but I am married to him now and—'

'And you love him,' Kate finished for her, squeezing her hand. 'Otherwise, you would not have chosen to elope with him. You should remember that, John.'

'I do not blame you, Mary,' John leaned forward and touched her hand.

Her father sat in the far corner. 'You love him... even knowing he lied to you.'

'I cannot choose to love or not, Papa. I cannot simply stop the emotions, and he is not all bad. He still says he loves me too.'

John made a disparaging sound.

'You may tell him, I will give him a chance to prove himself worthy of you,' her father said. 'But as I told him yesterday, if he does one thing to harm you...' He left the threat hanging in the air.

What else had her father said to Andrew yesterday? Had he been making threats and accusations when the two of them went to buy the special licence for their marriage? Was that why Andrew stormed off when she took her father's side? Was that the reason he had been so angry with her?

When he had apologised this morning, Andrew said he was angry with John and her father and taken it out on her.

2

At half past the hour of ten in the evening, Drew sauntered into the Everetts' drawing room. Conveniently it was the supper hour.

Mary's absence had tugged at him all evening, like the pull of a magnet. He wanted to be near her, no matter that he would have to endure the presence of her brother and father. He had decided to brave it for the benefit of his beautiful wife's company. Of course, London's high society, the ton, would observe the bruise on his chin and his flourishing black eye; but it would be Pembroke and Marlow who bore the embarrassment of that. A quarter of the room had seen it yesterday anyway, when he drove Mary from Pembroke's town mansion to his bachelor apartment in The Albany. So, everyone in the room probably already knew about their marriage and his bruises and had probably assumed her family were unhappy with the match.

He had brought his friends with him, to shield him somewhat from society's attention. They were easily persuaded when he advised them that Mary's friend, Miss Smithfield, would be present. The lady that Drew's best friend, Lord Peter Brooke, had in mind for a wife. They walked into the house in their usual pack, like wolves. But once inside he separated from them. They headed towards the buffet. He searched for Mary.

'Drew.' A hand touched his arm.

He turned. 'Caro. How are you?' He always had time for his younger sister. 'Is something wrong?'

Her lips lifted into a warm smile as he studied her face, checking. There were no bruises beneath her powder today. Her palm rested against the bruised side of his face. 'What have you been up to? I hear you married Miss Marlow.'

'I did.' His lips would have lifted to a grin, but that hurt so his smile fell.

'Do you think yourself in love?' she whispered, her eyes studying his expression. 'I have never seen you at a musical evening before.'

'I do not think it, I *am* in love. However, Mary... After her family had words with her, is not so sure.'

'I wish you happy.'

'Thank you. But you should be happy too. I have the money to smuggle you away from your husband now, Caro.'

'I will never get away. He would find me.'

'No. I will buy a property where he will not look.'

'I cannot—'

'Caro. You must come into supper with me.'

They both turned, responding to the sharp, fierce, command. The Marquis of Kilbride approached to retrieve and control Caro.

She glanced back at Drew, fear in her eyes, as she nodded before turning away.

Drew sighed as she left him. For years he had not been able to help her, but now he would insist she ran away from her vicious bully of a husband.

Mary was standing among her usual knot of friends. It took

her all of seconds to spot him, and her mouth dropped open a little as she did so, unable to hide her shock. She smiled.

He smiled too. It did not look as if he were an unwelcome shock.

She turned to him as he neared. He gently held up her hand, bowed over it and kissed her satin-covered knuckles, then tipped over her hand and kissed her wrist above her glove.

When he straightened, he said, 'Good evening, wife.'

'I did not expect you.' She sounded stunned.

'I did not intend coming, but I missed you, so I changed my mind.'

A blush flared on her pale cheeks but if his arrival had embarrassed her, she hid it well and turned to introduce him to her friends. He had watched her with these young people for two seasons. They were only a few years younger than him but they all seemed so naïve, it was as if he had a dozen years on them not four or five.

They stared at him as if he were an oddity. He forced himself to be polite, and all the while Mary's fingers rested on his left forearm.

It felt as though her fingers clasped his heart.

When the introductions were complete, he turned to her. 'Have you eaten?'

'Not yet.'

'Then may I escort you to fetch some supper before the performance recommences?'

'Thank you, yes.'

She excused herself from her dull friends and walked away with him.

Drew's world flooded with a light only Mary could bring to it.

He helped her fill a plate, positioning himself so Mary could not see his friends clustered in a corner about poor Miss Smith-field and another young woman.

He led Mary to an empty table, but within minutes her cousin, Lady Eleanor, and her husband, Lord Harry Nettleton, joined them. Drew knew Lord Nettleton, though not well. Mary's mother and her aunt, Lady Wiltshire, then also orientated in their direction. So, therefore, did Mary's father and her uncle, Lord Wiltshire, the Duke of Arundel. The Duke gave Drew a measuring stare as he withdrew a chair for his wife.

When Pembroke saw Drew seated at the table, though, he turned to another table, taking his Duchess with him.

The final seats were occupied by another aunt and uncle, the Duke of Bradford and his wife.

When the time for introductions came, Drew cringed internally, his instincts prickling with a desire to run. This was an endurance test, but his determination was set. He would survive it for Mary. Let her family believe whatever they wanted to about him, and say whatever they would. He knew his reputation, but he also knew the truth.

Her father watched, hawk-like, as Drew answered questions and participated in the conversation as best he could, while Mary glowed beside him, like the sun, burning bright and keeping him warm. It was novel indeed to have watched her seated among her family like this, as an outsider looking in, and now to be within.

He actually began enjoying himself as Lord Nettleton shared a joke and the table broke into laughter. Then the bell rang, indicating the performance was about to recommence.

He had never attended a musical evening. He expected to be bored.

He rose and offered his arm to Mary, then led her back into the drawing room among her family. Mary's father sat on the other side of her, and Drew had her sister-in-law, the Duchess of

Pembroke, beside him. The lady he had flippantly propositioned once.

She kept her distance, leaning against Pembroke's shoulder, her hand clasped in Pembroke's, resting on his thigh. The man must have some redeeming qualities because she still looked in love with him.

Drew lifted his right leg, his body jolting a little as the rib her father had broken jarred, and set his ankle on the opposite knee. Then he reached for Mary's hand and wove his fingers through hers, leaving their joined hands in her lap.

'I did not think you were attending,' Pembroke whispered in Drew's direction.

Drew turned, lifting one eyebrow. He was here to be with Mary, he had no intention of making the place a battleground. 'I changed my mind.'

'John.' Pembroke's wife dug an elbow into her husband's ribs.

Smirking, Drew looked away. At least Pembroke's wife was sensible. Mary squeezed Drew's hand. Drew looked to see the tone he had heard in the Duchess's voice reflected in Mary's expression – she was annoyed with her half-brother too. He smiled, pleased with his restraint. He had come here to continue making peace with her, not start another fight.

He faced forward as a harpist began to strum.

Mary's shoulder touched his arm, her delicate weight leaning upon him.

A tight constraint clenched about his heart. It hurt that she did not believe he loved her, that she thought him a rogue, a wastrel and a fortune-hunter. He had come to prove those things were not true. He wanted her to trust him, to rely on him, to lean on him always, just like this.

When the harpist sang, the music reeled him in. Perhaps his awakening emotions gave him new ears. Music had never touched him before. The woman's voice was haunting. A piano concerto followed, and then the night's entertainment was closed by a soprano, who again was outstanding.

Letting go of Mary's hand, he applauded the performers with the rest.

When everyone stood to leave, Drew possessively rested his hand at Mary's waist as they filed from the row. Her father looked down at his hand, then up to Drew's face, but he said nothing.

'Will you ride home with us, Lord Framlington?' the Duchess of Pembroke asked. 'We were to take Mary, so we could take you both.'

Her words were an olive branch. He was willing to accept it but he wished Mary to be reliant on him not her family. He turned, smiled and bowed to Pembroke's wife. 'Your Grace, thank you, but I shall take my wife home. We can hire a hansom.'

Pembroke eyed Drew with a hard glare.

Ignoring the judgemental look, Drew turned to Mary. 'I will say goodnight to my friends, then we will go. Please excuse me a moment.'

Her eyes opened wider at the mention of his friends but she did not deter him, merely nodded and turned to her father.

Drew could not see them in the room, and Miss Smithfield stood with her parents. He presumed they were in the room set up for cards and headed there.

'I cannot believe Mary would take a man like Lord Drew Framlington willingly. Do you think he forced her?'

Looking sideways, Drew sought the owner of that voice. It came from a group of young people, some of whom were Mary's friends. They had not noticed him.

'Emily said she ran away with him, and now Mary told her not to trust any of his friends, or even Lord Framlington himself.'

'Have you seen his black eye? It's a beaut. I heard Marlow did it. He caught them up, knocked the hell out of Lord Framlington and forced him to wed her there and then.'

The last came from a tall young gentleman – one of Lord Farquhar's boys. Drew knew the family, far too well. His mother was a friend of Drew's mother – and that was not a good recommendation.

The woman clutching Farquhar's arm caught Drew's eye and her jaw dropped open.

'Do you think he intended marrying her?'

'Of course he did, at some point,' Farquhar answered. 'He was after her fortune.'

His lady companion pulled on Farquhar's arm.

Half of Drew wanted to laugh, the other half would willingly knock the boy down...

The first woman who had spoken squealed, her hand covering her mouth as she noticed Drew approaching. Farquhar turned scarlet.

'Your voices are carrying,' Drew stated in a hard, measured voice. 'If you malign a man, at least have the guts to do so to his face and not behind his back. And if you'd care to observe what you risk, you may meet me at Manton's practice range on the morrow, Farquhar, to see how well I shoot. Or, you may prefer, to simply not speak ill of myself or my wife—'

'We were not—' one of the young women began.

'My dear, I heard...' Drew stared at her, 'and I'll not have it repeated.' His gaze travelled about the group. They were all cowed.

And these are her friends... Drew scoffed as he walked on.

'Can you believe he—'

'He is still in earshot, Bethany, and even if he were not, I do not fancy giving him cause to call me out.' Farquhar at least had received and understood the message.

Drew saw his friends leaving the card room.

'Gentlemen!' Drew called. 'Have you had a good night?'

'A very good one for me,' Mark answered, patting a pocket.

'A not so good one for Peter,' Harry said.

Drew looked at Peter. 'Ah, well, you can afford it at least.'

'I played ill, I am out of sorts. Your wife has shattered my hopes of the fair Miss Smithfield.'

Drew laughed. 'Did you have any honest, decent hopes, you scoundrel?'

'I do not recall even mentioning decent or honest, but whatever my intent, my hopes are dashed. Your wife warned her off.'

'Ah. I can explain that. She was not asleep last night, she heard you talking. I am afraid you shot yourself in the foot.'

'Bloody hell!' Peter barked with a laugh, drawing eyes from about the room.

'Bloody hell indeed. I took a battering for not being the author of those love letters...'

'Then we must apologise in person,' Harry stated with bravado.

'Yes,' Peter agreed. 'You have to let us speak with her, you cannot keep your wife from us. Or are you ashamed of us now you are rich?'

'I am still not as rich as you, Peter,' Drew responded, 'and therefore why would I have reason to cut you? Come, I will let you speak with her, as long as you behave.'

'I am wounded,' Peter said theatrically, pressing his hand to his chest over his heart. 'Do I not always behave?'

'No,' Drew answered, looking at them all, 'we do not, but I must start behaving now I am married, and you must respect my wife when you speak to her, understood?'

They laughed, not taking him seriously in the least.

He turned, with a sigh, wondering if he had just cast his

marriage a death sentence. But these were his friends, who were more like brothers to him than his brothers had ever been. They were, and always would be, a part of his life. Mary had to accept that, it was not negotiable.

Her eyebrows lifted as she saw them coming and her skin pinked. Clearly she did not wish to meet them, but there was a point to be made here. He would do much for her, but he would not reject his friends.

The Dukes of Bradford and Arundel stared as Drew and his friends neared; his pack of wolves approaching the Pembroke pride of lions.

Drew beckoned Mary, to bring her away from them. He did not fancy a full-blown war breaking out in the Everetts' drawing room.

She came, although she looked nervous, but obviously his turning up here had gone some way towards building bridges as opposed to hurdles.

He hoped this did not knock them down.

'Sweetheart,' he stated as she came over, 'my friends wish to apologise, they did not mean to offend you last night.' She blushed harder as he took her elbow and turned her to the others.

'Lady Framlington. Felicitations on your marriage,' Peter stated with a brief bow.

'Lord Brooke.' She bobbed a slight curtsy. 'Thank you.'

Drew doubted she was thankful at all.

'I am pleased the prose worked.' Peter claimed one of her hands and lifted it to his lips. 'And glad you deemed our dear friend worthy.'

Discomfort rippled through Drew; he did not like Peter touching her.

Mary withdrew her fingers before Peter could kiss them. 'Your prose was very good, Lord Brooke, but I have told you before, I do not value false flattery.'

'But my dear, it was never false.' Peter couldn't help flirting with any woman.

The hairs on the back of Drew's neck prickled because this woman was not any woman, she was his.

'Now if you would simply unsay whatever it is you said to your friend—'

'Congratulations, Lady Framlington,' Harry interrupted.

'You have my good wishes too.' Mark vied for her attention as he and Harry bowed, both reaching for her hand. Mark claimed it first and pressed a kiss on the back of it, then passed her hand to Harry.

'And Miss Smithfield...' Peter prodded.

'Will have nothing more to do with you, I am afraid, Lord Brooke, if she is sensible.'

'And from that I conclude you think yourself not sensible.' Peter's eyebrows lifted as he glanced in Drew's direction. 'So, all is not roses in heaven then, Fram.' Peter slapped Drew's shoulder. 'But you are still rich...'

Drew shrugged. He would not discuss his issues with them. 'But not as rich as you,' he quipped again, to hide his unease.

'May we call on you at Drew's?' Mark asked Mary.

'You have such lovely eyes,' Harry complimented.

Drew stepped closer to her. 'No one is to call unless invited. Mary will not wish to be hounded by you reprobates.'

'And if you do call, she is likely to be out!' The deep pitch came from behind Drew.

Marlow.

Drew turned.

The Dukes of Arundel and Bradford stood at her father's right and left shoulders.

Would Mary be the rope in a tug of war every day of their marriage?

Perhaps, Drew should have stayed away and left her to her family here.

At least his friends recognised the moment to bow out. They withdrew, rather than begin a brawl, laughing, presumably at Lord Marlow and his in-laws.

'Why would you subject my daughter to their lechery?' Marlow accused when Peter, Harry and Mark were barely out of earshot.

'Papa...' Mary touched her father's arm.

'Mary.' Drew held out his hand. This was another moment when she must make a choice. He was all or he was nothing to her. 'I will take you home.'

To his irritation she hesitated. Drew's jaw clenched and he lifted his hand higher. She had taken a vow to obey him but he wanted her to come because she wished to.

Her pale blue gaze met his, just as Pembroke joined the altercation. Her father was the brother of an Earl, but her wider family commanded influence across the whole of society through her mother's connections.

'I will go home with Andrew, Papa. John.' She looked at them, and her uncles. 'I'll call on you tomorrow, Papa.'

When she took Drew's hand, he held hers tightly, emotion wrapping about his heart. 'Good evening, Lord Marlow, Your Graces,' Drew said, before turning away with Mary.

He strode from the room briskly, meaning Mary had to hurry to keep up.

They were watched by other guests the entire length of their flight. When they reached the door, he could not help himself, he looked back and glared at everyone who still stared.

The men of her family had huddled together in the centre of

the room, forming a conference, undoubtedly planning what to do about him.

Fuck them!

He obtained Mary's shawl and his hat and had a footman send a stable boy to find a hansom carriage. The same footman held the carriage door as Drew handed Mary in.

When he climbed in beside her, she had pressed herself into the far corner of the small two-seater carriage and looked through the window.

After the door shut, the carriage lurched into motion.

She would make a wonderful subject for a portrait in the lantern light of the carriage, staring at nothing in the darkness, her face reflected in the glass.

'Did your friends come just to play their games with Emily?' she asked the window. 'Could you not have stopped them?'

He sighed. The ground he had gained earlier was lost.

She looked at him. 'I was pleased to see you until you said they were with you.' Her voice grew in strength. 'How can you condone their behaviour?'

Her condemnation of them was condemnation of him, and she knew it. 'Lord Brooke is not such a bad catch, he is remarkably wealthy.'

'But we both know he is not thinking of marriage, is he?'

'If she is properly chaperoned, what does that matter? You never know, he might fall for her.' The last was a quip at his own expense, which of course she would not understand as she did not believe he had fallen.

'But we both know chaperones can be avoided.' Her pitch soured as she shot a wisecrack back at him. 'I suppose you have all played these games a hundred times.'

Drew turned, one knee lifting onto the seat between them as he faced her, his arm stretching across the squabs behind her shoulders. His body jolted with the pain from the rib her father had broken – when he discovered the deeply in love runaways they were two days ago.

'So we are back to how many, are we? Well, for your information, you are the first woman I have courted, and the first woman I have known who had any need of chaperones, and for all Peter may play around and act the fool, he has never courted a virgin before either. Judge them how you like, but at least my friends are loyal. I caught yours gossiping about you.'

How did she have the power to make him feel like a belligerent child? *Because I love her.* This was what love did. It made you weak and miserable. This was why his heart had forgotten love as a child. But he was not giving in yet, he was fighting for her.

'I suppose you frightened my friends into silence.'

'Do I frighten you?'

'Yes. Sometimes. When you feel threatened and become angry with me.'

Her admission shocked him. His anger fled instantly. 'Then, I am sorry. I do not mean to make you afraid.'

His hand lifted, needing to hold her, and without his urging, as though they had the same desire in the same moment, she rose and turned to sit on his lap. Her arms reached about his neck, but then a sob sounded against his shoulder. 'I do not want to argue.'

Damn it. He leaned back further, breaking the embrace to look at her face. Tears sparkled on her cheeks.

'How else do I make you feel?' he asked, wanting her to say something good.

'Sad. I wonder if you will ever love me, or I will ever understand you.'

'I do love you,' he answered.

Their lives were worlds apart. She could never walk in his

path but he could walk in hers. He should try. The onus to make their marriage work rested on him. 'When you go to Pembroke's house tomorrow, I will come.' If nothing else it would stop her family influencing her in his absence.

'Do you think that wise? Papa is still angry with you.'

'That is the reason I should go.' The familiar surge of love for her raced through his blood and his gaze dropped to her lips.

She smiled, then, her fingers slipping into his hair, she brought his mouth to hers.

When the carriage pulled to a halt, they were only prevented from being thrown onto the floor by Drew bracing his feet hard and holding onto her.

He moved her from his lap as the hatch below the driver's seat slid open. 'We're 'ere, sir, ma'am.'

Drew freed the lock and pushed the door open. He climbed out, helped Mary down, then paid the driver.

A night porter opened the front door of The Albany. As Mary stepped over the threshold, awe stole his breath away. He could not quite believe she was here. A lopsided smile tilting his lips, he bent and caught her up in his arms. She held his shoulders. 'Andrew!'

'I omitted to do this before, didn't I? It was remiss of me. A bridegroom should carry his wife across their threshold.'

The doorman grunted his amusement, stepping aside, so Drew could carry her past him and up the stairs.

The pain in his rib hurt like hell, but despite Marlow's bitter words and violence, Drew was going to make his marriage happy. He would prove them wrong.

3

Mary laughed, looking into Andrew's eyes as he carried her up the stairs. The gesture was a day late, but it touched her heart. She was glad he had come tonight, though, she was unsure why he had. Yet even if he had come because Lord Brooke wished to chase after Emily, Andrew had sat with her.

She had never seen him at such an event before. He even ate among her family. But then he brought his horrible friends to speak to her...

At least Emily was safely chaperoned – as long as she did not fall for Lord Brooke's charm, as Mary had fallen for Andrew's.

That charm flowed about her as he carried her upstairs.

Earlier, while they played chess and dressed together, she glimpsed how their marriage might be, and tonight she felt like one of a couple.

She watched his face, illuminated by the lanterns in the hall.

Her husband was a complex man. 'You value your friends, don't you,' she said, as they reached the landing.

'Yes, they are like brothers.'

'How long have you known them?'

'Since school.' As they reached the door of his apartment, he lowered her feet to the ground, so he could withdraw a key from his pocket.

'Kate, my sister-in-law's, brother, was John's best friend at school.'

'I know. He is your brother's man of business. I discovered that when he paid me your dowry.'

'Kate used to play with John and Philip. I was too young.'

He kicked the door open with his foot, picked her up again and carried her over the threshold of his two-room bachelor apartment.

One of the service maids must have been into the room. A single oil lamp had been left burning by the door.

He lowered her legs with a tenderness that spoke of the love he said he felt – it made her want to believe him. She had thought his choice of friends was evidence that John's depiction of Andrew's character was right. However, if John was wrong about Andrew, perhaps she was wrong about his friends. Perhaps they also hid their good sides behind bravado...

'Should I get to know your friends, and judge them for myself?'

'Ah, so are they to be on a suspended sentence? I would like it if you did know them better.'

Andrew was funny when he wished to be, and kind... and he had no reason to pretend he was in love now he had her money.

'And my judgement, Mary? Where do I stand?' His hazel eyes studied her.

She turned her back and removed her shawl. 'You are my husband...' She lay her shawl over a chair. 'Do you want me to pour you a drink?' She would not admit she loved him when she was not sure what he felt.

From his expression he appeared to be trying to solve a puzzle. 'That is a very wifely offer. Yes, I will have a drink.'

'Brandy?' she asked.

'Yes, please. It is all I have, anyway. From a bottle my rich friend, Peter, bought. We will buy our own brandy and whatever you like to drink tomorrow.'

While she opened the decanter and poured the brandy into a glass, he removed his hat, gloves and evening coat.

When she put the decanter down, he stood behind her and his hands slipped about her waist, embracing her, as his lips kissed her shoulder.

'Do you want me to ring for a kettle of water for tea?' he asked.

She turned, forcing him to step back. She held out his drink. 'No, the maids will be in bed, I would not want to wake them. I am not thirsty anyway, and besides, you do not even have a teapot.'

'Another item to add to our shopping list.' He accepted the glass. 'Have I taken you from heaven, Mary, and brought you here to share hell with me?'

Sometimes he said the strangest things, but the words proved that he was leagues deep. Her fingertips touched the bruise about his eye that had turned from red to yellow now. 'Does it hurt?'

'Somewhat. So do not touch it.'

Her hand lowered.

'Come and sit in a chair with me.' He put the glass on the games table, beside an armchair, sat down and patted his thighs, his roguish smile playing on his lips.

She sat sideways on his lap, smiling at his foolishness as she draped an arm around his shoulders.

He reclaimed his drink and sipped from the glass.

She pressed a kiss on the bruise on his jaw.

His smile broadened and he touched a fingertip to his lips. 'It hurts here, too.'

'Did Papa and John hurt you badly when they hit you?'

'Now she asks...' His voice rang deep. 'I am sure you do not care if they did. I believe the word is comeuppance.'

'You were a day late in carrying me over the threshold. I am a couple of days late in asking if you were hurt. We are even.'

His fingers brushed strands of her hair back from her face, while he sipped more brandy.

'You did not hit them...' *Why had she not noted that before?* He had not fought against them. He had accepted their anger. *Comeuppance* – if he respected their anger, that was not the action of a bad, or a deceitful, man.

'That would have been unjust, don't you think? If I was your papa, or your brother, I'd have punched me, too. In fact, if anyone took you from me now, there would be carnage.'

Her fingers pressed against his midriff, as she moved to get up.

'Ow! God.'

She stopped moving. 'What is it?'

'Your dear papa broke my rib, Mary.'

'You did not say.' She stood up, not wanting to hurt him.

'When was the moment to mention it? I can take a punch. I am not complaining. After all, I did seduce you...' He watched her as he spoke, as though judging her response. Deviltry flashed in his eyes as he sipped the brandy. 'I seduced you because I want you, Mary. I am guilty of that. I should have asked for your father's consent, but we both know I would not have received it, and... At some point along our path, I fell in love with you. I did not lie about that.

'Yes, I urged you to marry me. But you came with me by choice...' He lifted his hand. 'Come back, sit down, you were keeping me warm.'

'I will hurt your rib.'

'I will worry about my rib. Come on, sweetheart, sit and talk to me.'

'We are talking, but I do not think that is what you wish to do.'

His smile tilted sideways, turning her stomach to fluid. 'Ah, you got me. Come and give me a kiss, then.'

His words pulled her physically. It was hopeless pretending she did not want to be with him. She told Emily to learn from her mistakes, yet *he* had just admitted seducing her and she was letting him do it again.

She wanted to trust him, but he had not told her about the indecent offer he'd made to Kate... She had a sudden desire to be in control of her marriage and she knew a way to take control of him. She had learned his body's reactions to her touch in the summerhouse, when he had been in the midst of seducing her.

She raised the hem of her dress, turning predator, lifting it above her knees, flashing the ribbons holding up her stockings.

He choked on his brandy when he realised what she meant to do, wiped his lips with the side of his hand, then put the glass down and moved his legs together, so her knees could fit either side.

She straddled him, in an intimate position, the skirt of her raised dress tumbling over their thighs.

'You can get rid of these for a start,' he said, catching hold of her hand then tugging off her glove. He smiled slyly, as he dropped her glove on the table beside his glass, lifting her hand and slipping one of her fingers into his mouth. He sucked it gently.

But this was about her taking control, not submissively being done to. She wanted to seduce him. She wanted him to know she had some control in their marriage.

She reclaimed her finger, leaned forward, her palm bracing

his nape, and kissed him. *Comeuppance.* It felt like exquisite justice.

When her lips left his, he smiled.

Her fingers released the buttons of his waistcoat, as he tugged his shirt free from the waistband of his trousers.

'Let me.' She knocked his hand aside. He flinched.

She had forgotten his broken rib.

'Don't stop,' he told her. 'Just be careful.'

'Let me see?' She pushed his waistcoat off his shoulders, as he leaned forward so she could take that and his shirt off.

The vivid bruise stained half his side and looked like a messy artist's pallet of reds, yellows and dark purple. Her fingertips gently touched his side. 'You should have asked me to bandage it for you.'

'You would not have bandaged me up at that inn.' Petulance crept into his voice. 'Not after your father and brother convinced you I was evil.'

'I never thought you were evil. But you do have a devil in you that likes to hit out.' He had not fought against their punches or their accusations when they were found at the inn, but he had used words to hurt them. 'I know you asked my father about my dowry, and whether you should call him Papa, to upset him.'

A chuckle rumbled from his throat, then an expression said that too had hurt his rib. 'Yes. But I only hit out at people who hit out at me. Enough talking,' he said, in a deeper tone.

'Your rib, Andrew...'

'Darling, physical intimacy is the best painkiller. Forget my rib. I am half naked and beneath you.'

She shook her head and pushed away the hand that lifted. 'No. I am in control tonight.' She had contemplated this when he used his mouth and teeth on her. He had reacted once when she touched his tip accidentally. It would put her in complete control. The great seducer – toppled by his own tricks.

If her marriage was to work it would be with her as an equal, and she knew exactly how to make her husband pay attention. If she took control of him physically, he would view her differently.

She pressed her palms on the arms of the chair, lifted her legs.

'Don't go—'

She pressed her fingertip to his lips to silence him. Then lowered herself to the floor, kneeling in front of him. His eyes burned bright, gleaming in the lamplight as she released the buttons securing his flap.

This would change the balance of everything between them...

* * *

Drew forgot his pain – forgot about anything but this beautiful woman he loved. This was the prim Miss Mary Marlow. His fingernails scratched into the arms of the chair. No, this was Lady Framlington. Perhaps his name had tainted her.

This morning, she cried when he made love to her. This evening...

'You do not have to do this.' His voice came out as a whisper. His arousal was agony.

She ignored him.

When her lips encompassed him, he gritted his teeth and his fingers wrapped around the arms of the chair and clung to it. As she caressed him, with her lips, mouth and tongue, he slipped the comb out of her hair, set it aside and pulled out the pins, one by one. A stream of ebony hair fell across his legs as he removed each pin.

'Mary, darling,' he groaned, threading his fingers through her hair.

She focused on what she was doing, ignoring his responses.

'Mary...' His hips took up her rhythm – claiming what she gave. 'Mary.' He was going to come undone. His hands clasped her shoulders, urging her to stop. He could not bear it.

She would not stop.

He shut his eyes, gritted his teeth, and fought against it... *Damn it. 'Mary!'* He came into her mouth in an overwhelming rush, his hands clasping fistfuls of her hair.

A deep breath pulled into his lungs and his fingers slipped free from her hair as sanity returned. He could not believe his respectable wife had done this to him.

She stood. 'Now you know how it feels to be seduced,' she said, and left him in the chair, hot and drained.

Lord... She could seduce him any time she wanted to.

'Mary?' He wanted to rise and follow her but his limbs refused to obey.

She walked into the bedroom, without looking back at him.

Had that been a lesson? If so, he had not learned it.

After a moment, he secured his flap and followed her.

She was undressing. 'Mary, I love—'

'Don't spoil it,' she answered bluntly, glancing at him.

He crossed the room and caught her arm to make her listen. 'I do love you.'

Tears glistened in her eyes. 'You do not have to lie any more, you have my money. I know you like me, that is enough.'

'I am not lying!' How could she have done that, then act like it meant nothing? Other women had done the same of course, but it had never felt like that, because love changed everything. Of course, she was innocent, and she would not know the difference.

That rigid gaze of hers, that she had learned from the Dukes in her family, said, *let go of me.* He did so.

He carried her up here thinking they could be happy, yet, already she had discovered he was a selfish rake who could be manipulated with sex. There was a desire to go in search of his friends and sink his sorrows in his cups. They would still be in the clubs.

She sniffed as her dress fell to the floor and she began awkwardly trying to unlace her corset.

She was crying.

He was a fool. He kept making her unhappy. He did not know how to love her. *But* he would not leave her alone, because leaving her would make her think he did not love her.

He held her, enveloping her in a gesture of kindness, because he did care. She turned into the embrace. One hand stroked her hair, the other her back. She was his everything, from alpha to omega, his first and last, no matter what else. 'It will be good between us. It will. I promise.'

Her arms wrapped about his midriff, holding tight and jarring his broken rib.

'I will release your laces, then you can get into bed.'

The only way he knew how to show love was with his body, he had to make her believe.

4
_____

When Mary woke the next morning, Andrew was not in bed. The room smelt delicious, of bacon, fresh bread, brewing coffee and warm chocolate. She got up and wrapped her shawl around her shoulders, her hair loose and wild. She had not plaited it last night because they made love again. Her stomach rumbled as she walked to the bedroom door.

Andrew must have risen and washed quietly, she could see the shaving brush and razor in the dressing room were wet.

Mary opened the door, rubbing sleep from one eye, her cheeks still warm from the bed.

Andrew stood beside the table that was full of plates of food. 'Good morning. Come and sit down. I ordered chocolate for you to drink, as well as the meal.'

She sat at the table in her nightdress with her favourite paisley shawl draped over her shoulders.

He poured her chocolate while she buttered bread, the soles of her bare feet resting on the rung of the chair.

He sat in the chair closest to her.

They ate in silence. What she did last night, to teach Andrew a lesson, had made him think. She knew when he made love to her in bed later, there was repentance in his tenderness.

It made her think about things too – about how happy John and Kate were; how happy all her married cousins were with their husbands. She wanted a marriage like theirs. That is why she cried last night.

She looked at him. His cheeks reddened with a blush, then his gaze dropped to his food, as though he were unable to look at her this morning.

He was trying to prove that he cared again today, by ordering breakfast to please her.

'Will you ride in Hyde Park this morning?' she asked.

He looked up and shook his head. 'It is raining.'

She looked at the window. It was only drizzling. 'That is not rain. You cannot even call it a shower. It is falling dew. I have been out riding in a deluge with Robbie. Riding in the rain is fun. Can we not go together? I have my habit in my trunks.'

'And when I take you to your papa's later and you have caught a chill, it will be me he blames.'

'Papa knows me well enough to realise who to blame, and I have a far better constitution than to catch a chill from a pathetic attempt at rainfall such as that.'

His eyes shone with amusement. 'I ride my carriage horses. I have no others. They are spirited…' he warned.

'I can handle a spirited horse. I would be bored on a tame animal.'

He laughed. 'Well, that explains much.'

'Can we ride then?'

'Yes, we will ride.'

'Thank you.'

She smiled through the rest of their breakfast, as they talked about things they would add to their shopping list to make his rooms more comfortable for her.

When she had finished eating, she said, 'Will you help me dress?'

'Yes. Find your riding habit, I shall be there in a moment.'

Their ride was exhilarating, the fine rain only served to keep her cool. Though it dampened her hair and habit, the rain meant they had Hyde Park virtually to themselves, so they rode across the grass at a gallop, laughing and shouting. She felt as happy as when she rode at home with Robbie.

Andrew's horses were fast. She rode Athena, he Hera. There was no need for a whip to make Athena run. The horses had wonderful temperaments, because he spoiled them with affection. When he greeted them in the stables, he petted them and whispered to them. Every day she learned something new about her husband. He had told her his horses were important, now she knew they were as important as his friends.

She watched him as they rode back at a trot, side by side. His eyes were gleaming. His wet riding coat clung to his body, but he did not seem to care. He sat a horse well, his strong thighs and calves pressing against the animal's flanks, his back straight and his hold on the reins relaxed. If she saw him from a distance across a field, she would think him handsome, without even seeing his face. He radiated strength and masculinity.

A smile lifted her lips – *it seems I like spirited men, as much as spirited horses.*

When they reached the stables, he swung down from the saddle, dropping to the cobbles. Then came to help her dismount. His hands held her waist.

She rested her hands on his shoulders. 'I understand another fragment of you, Andrew Framlington.'

'Do you?' He took her weight and lifted her down. 'Should I be concerned?'

'You are an escapist.' They faced one another, her hands still on his shoulders, his lingering at her waist. 'I have found you out. You hunted an heiress rather than settled on an occupation, so you could ride not work.'

He smiled. 'I suppose that is not a compliment, but you can hardly judge, you are the same. I would guess you would rather be riding than sewing in a parlour.'

'Guilty.' She laughed.

He released her, reached past her and patted Athena's side.

'I know something else about you too; you like people to think you don't care about anything. But you have always cared for something or someone.'

His gaze met hers, and his smile twisted as a groom led the horses away. 'Pray, do not tell a soul.' His hand caught hold of hers. 'Come, let us eat luncheon before we go to your brother's.'

5

When Drew arrived at the Duke of Pembroke's town house two hours later, he felt like a king because Mary was in charity with him.

They had walked there, because the rain had ceased and they both liked exercise.

She had donned a bright indigo blue day dress, beneath a navy spencer. Her bonnet was also navy and sported a small clutch of silk bluebells above her right ear. She looked charming, and he was not the only one who thought so, many men noticed her as they walked. Even the attention she drew had not dampened his mood. When they eloped, he told her his horses were the most valuable things he owned. They were not now, she was priceless.

The front door opened. Pembroke's imperious butler stared at him.

'Mr Finch,' Mary acknowledged. The man stepped back, letting Mary pass and with her fingers around Drew's arm, she took him with her.

'Is everyone in the upstairs sitting room?'

Drew's discomfort rose like mercury in a thermometer. He doubted he would be welcome here, but he was here for Mary's sake.

The butler bowed towards Mary. 'Yes, ma'am. They are. Shall I show you up?' He looked down his nose towards Drew.

Drew's devil spiked. 'Don't worry, Finch, we can take ourselves up.'

'May I take your outdoor garments, my lady?' the butler offered, ignoring Drew.

'Thank you.' Mary smiled as she pulled the ribbons of her bonnet loose. 'I am still not used to being called a lady, Finch.'

Drew took her bonnet and handed it to the butler, along with his hat and gloves. Then helped her remove her spencer, lifting it from her shoulders. He lay that across the butler's forearms as his hands were full. He smiled, enjoying putting the butler in his place.

A moment later they climbed the stairs; she eager, he reluctant but enduring.

The upstairs landing was lined by two dozen intimidating portraits of Mary's ancestors and artefacts gathered on grand tours. They reminded him of her family's wealth.

Voices travelled from an open door. Mary's pace quickened.

A drowning sensation took hold. *Why did I say I would come?*

'You are an escapist...' The word he would use was still coward...

He set his jaw and walked on, focusing on the hand on his arm. He was here for her.

When they entered the drawing room, he realised he had been ambushed. The room contained her mother and father, her half-brother and his wife, and her aunts and uncles; the Dukes and Duchesses of Arundel and Bradford, and the Earl of Barrington, Marlow's brother, and his wife, also some of her cousins.

As Mary led him to a sofa, judgemental looks were cast across the room, in silent speech.

There were lots of children in the room too. Some seated on the floor, playing and giggling, some on the knees of their mothers, and others occupying chairs among the adults.

A sharp pain impaled his heart – the scene was something from fiction books. A fairy tale.

'Good day, everyone. Andrew has come to meet you.'

As Mary began to make introductions, Drew's jaw set firm.

It was hard to tell which child belonged to whom, so many of them bore the Pembrokes' dark hair and pale eyed colouring.

Mary completed an introduction.

Drew was too discombobulated to listen, but he knew the woman was Lady Wiltshire, Arundel's Duchess.

A circle of boys sat cross-legged in the far corner, contentedly playing cards with fish tokens. His brothers were never that good-humoured, and he was confined to the nursery until he boarded at school, out of sight and mind.

Lady Wiltshire bid two of the girls move from a sofa and make room for him and Mary to sit together. Then she offered him a cup of tea.

He sat in a daydream. This was his first experience of afternoon tea, let alone a happy family.

Mary's family laughed and chatted around him. He accepted a cup and saucer from her aunt but could not force any words of gratitude from his lips.

A girl who had got up to let him sit brought an embroidery hoop to show Mary, asking for her advice. The girl was her sister...

Drew felt as though he were looking into the room through a window.

Mary's sister glanced at him, before walking over to her mother.

'Mary!' A smaller girl with a ragdoll dangling from her hand rushed to Mary.

'Jemima!' Mary mimicked her excitement, caught her and lifted her onto her lap.

'You are my new brother, are you not?' Her small hand rested on his thigh.

His cup and saucer were balanced in his hand. He put the cup and saucer on a table beside the sofa, not knowing what to do. A lump in his throat made it difficult to breathe.

The little girl told Mary something about her doll.

Mary's fingers touched his arm for a moment, as though she understood. But she could not understand his childhood. It would be as inconceivable to her as this was to him.

A deep masculine laugh rang from the group of men. He stiffened, wondering if they were laughing at him.

Harry would be laughing his head off if he could see Drew sat there. Mark would have him sentenced to a madhouse in a week.

Drew cleared his throat, trying to shift the lump within it.

'Jemima,' Marlow's voice beckoned from across the room.

Drew looked up. The men had split up and were joining their wives.

The girl on Mary's lap slid off and ran to Marlow, with a bright smile. 'Papa.' She did not look at all scared of her father, despite the fact he had just barked at her.

He bent and picked her up, balancing her bottom on one forearm. She lifted her doll, saying something. He answered her, his free hand stroking her dark curls.

Drew looked away. He had glimpsed a bond that must hold between Mary and her father, too – years ago it would have been Mary in his arms.

No wonder Marlow had been so angry when Drew stole her away without so much as a by-your-leave.

Drew glanced about the room, as Mary talked to her aunt. His gaze collided with the Duchess of Pembroke's. She sat in a chair on his left, scarcely a yard away.

She looked at one of the older girls. 'Helen, dear, please offer people some of the cakes, would you?'

The girl, one of Marlow's, Drew would guess, and therefore another of Mary's sisters, did as she was asked.

In his family's home, that would have been one of the servants' tasks, but perhaps the children in this room were taught humility.

'I am pleased you came today.'

The Duchess's words made his muscles jump. If he had been holding his teacup, the liquid would have been in his lap. He looked at her but could not think of a word to say.

'You mustn't let my father-in-law or John put you off. If you prove your loyalty to Mary they will mellow.'

He did not care about them, but he had insulted her, he owed her an apology. 'Your Grace, I appreciate your...' *What?* He began again. 'I ought to... that is... I am sorry that I—'

She waved his words away. 'That is in the past, Lord Framlington,' she said, then stood up and walked away.

Did I upset her? His gaze followed her as she made her way to Pembroke, who was talking with the Earl of Barrington. Pembroke's arm lay about the Duchess's shoulders. He said something. She nodded. Then Pembroke looked at Drew, his gaze hardening with judgement.

Drew looked away, anger prickling.

Mary's father deposited Jemima on his wife's lap and kissed the child. When he straightened, as if sensing Drew's observation, he looked Drew's way. His expression hardened too. Then he looked at Mary.

'Mary, may I speak with you a moment?' *Alone.* He did not say the last word but his voice did, and Mary heard it, because she pressed a palm on Drew's thigh and stood.

Her father raised a hand, directing her towards a window seat on the opposite side of the room.

Cut off from her, Drew felt as isolated as he had as a child.

The sofa cushion beside him stirred. 'Forgive me, I should introduce myself, I am Mary's Aunt Jane, Lord Barrington's wife.'

He knew.

A movement on the window seat caught his attention. Mary's father touched a bruise on Mary's throat. It was only small, it had been left by Drew's fervent kisses last night.

'Mary is precious to us,' Lady Barrington said. 'Your marriage has shocked us all.'

He looked at her. 'It did not shock Mary. It was her choice. A choice she is old enough to make.'

'Yes. She is also a very kind and loving young lady. We hoped the right husband would give that back to her.'

'The right husband... Not me then?' Defiance sharpened his voice.

Was this the plot the men had been hatching in the corner? Remove Mary and send a woman to threaten him, so he would feel unable to defend himself. Clever.

'It could be you,' she answered. 'We shall see. I hope it is you, for Mary's sake.'

'Not mine...'

'At this moment in time, Lord Framlington, you have gained everything in your marriage, and Mary nothing. I think you have enough to be happy.'

His instinct was to stand up and leave, and to take Mary with him. But her family were important to her, and her Aunt Jane was right, he had gained everything; the least he could do for Mary was sit here and drink tea. 'Mary has gained one thing,' he said, though, unable to stop his indignation. 'Me. I know you think me lacking, but Mary does not.' *At least I hope that is true.*

His gaze returned to Mary. Her father held her hand as he spoke.

Lady Barrington touched Drew's arm. 'I hope you prove us wrong.' She stood and walked away.

Anger kicked his gut. No one cared about his happiness. Was it any wonder he had become a selfish, bitter man?

Mary's sister offered him a cake with an almond paste decoration. 'No, thank you, Helen.'

A moment later, one of the young boys, who Drew had a suspicion had been dared, stood in front of him with a pack of cards. 'Can I show you a trick I know?'

'Certainly...'

His next half an hour, until Mary returned to him and said they would leave, was spent with the boys who drifted closer and talked to him about horses and carriages, and other boyish things.

On their walk home, he tucked her arm under his and she held the sleeve of his coat at his forearm. He did not ask what her father had said, and she did not say. Before they left, he agreed to accompany Mary to a ball her family were attending, so whatever Marlow had said had changed nothing.

When they reached The Albany, he asked Joseph to order them a good dinner from Gunter's, then led her upstairs. 'Shall we play a few hands of cards or a game of chess?'

If he could learn to fit in among her family, their marriage might yet work...

6

Mary watched Andrew move the bishop across the board and take her knight.

She had discovered many elements of him, yet there seemed dozens more. He was like a puzzle – he could be gentle, kind and tolerant, but most of the time he was stubborn and defensive, and foolhardy with his friends.

Her father thought Andrew selfish, though pig-headed was the word he used. He asked if Andrew's friends came to the apartment. Then asked if Andrew was rough and touched her neck where Andrew had sucked her skin and left a bruise.

She swore Andrew was gentle and respectful and told him about their ride in the park, only to make her father annoyed that Andrew let her gallop on the wet grass.

She sighed. Something had disturbed Andrew this afternoon, though. He seemed confused among her family, as though he had no idea what to do or say.

Perhaps he did not know... The only thing he had told her about his family was that he neither liked them nor visited them.

'Have you spoken to your parents since we married?' She

lifted her bishop, moving it from the path of his. The marriage announcement was in the newspaper yesterday, so they must have seen it.

The muscles about his jaw tightened. 'My parents...' His pitch soured. He leaned to the side, grasped the neck of the bottle of champagne that had been delivered with their meal, and topped up her glass then his.

She guessed he filled their glasses to avoid answering.

'Will you introduce me?'

He looked at the board and slid a castle across the squares until it faced her king. 'Mate. No, I will not introduce you. Our marriage is nothing to do with my parents. Make your move?' He sipped champagne.

She moved her bishop to defend her king. 'I would like to meet them.'

'You would not.' He also made a defensive move.

'Let me decide.' She moved her queen in between two pawns. 'I do not want to bump into them and not know them; that would be embarrassing. Are you ashamed of me?'

His eyebrows lifted. 'I am ashamed of them.' He moved a pawn closer to her king.

'But we are married, I should at least know them.'

He did not answer. He sipped champagne, staring at the board, waiting for her to make her move.

Her fingers picked up her king and raised it close to her lips. His gaze followed the movement.

She smiled as his gaze struck hers. 'Are they in town?'

He shook his head, his expression not saying no, but telling her to stop.

* * *

They were in town. He saw them at one of the balls he attended while pursuing her, but Drew was not introducing her. She returned her king to its place and moved a pawn.

He moved his knight.

'I want to meet them.'

He ignored her, sipping champagne, and wishing she would give up. Today had been a good day, until she broached this untouchable subject.

'Andrew...'

'It is your move,' he said.

She moved her pawn from the line of his king and suddenly he realised she had trapped him.

'Checkmate.'

Damn, that was the end of distraction.

Conceding, he tipped his king over. She got up from her chair. He expected her to walk to the bedchamber, but instead she came to him and her fingers tilted up his chin, lifting his gaze to hers.

She smiled, coyly. 'Please, let me meet your parents. They must want to meet me.'

'They do not.' He lifted his chin away from her touch. 'Nor will they want to see me. So, no, we will not go.'

'Did you argue with them?' She picked up her glass, but did not sit down.

'Mary, I do not talk to them.' His temper increased by notches.

She was silent, as though she was working out a way to persuade him.

He sighed, drained his glass and stood. She needed something else to occupy her mind... 'Let us go to bed.'

An hour later, lying naked beside her, satisfied, his fingertips drew circles on the soft skin of her shoulder. 'You seem so fragile, yet you are not breakable at all, are you? I think there is steel beneath your skin, Mary.'

'I can be hurt, but probably not broken, because I have my family.'

Her answer kicked – it would have pleased him if she had said, *because I have you.*

While they made love, he felt her tender trust, yet now, again, when it was over, she did not believe in him.

'Introduce me to your parents, I want to meet them.'

Damn.

But... he thought... If it would convince her to believe in him, perhaps it was worth the risk. When she met them, she would know why he struggled with family bonds.

This was the worst thing she could ask of him.

Once it was over, his family would be forgotten and they could build their future.

She would see he had told the truth and might trust him more.

'Perhaps...' he answered. 'I will think about it.'

7

During breakfast Andrew was moody. Last night she believed he loved her. In their bed, he did not say, I love you, not even once, but she felt it. His touch was reverent.

She wanted to know everything about him, every side of him, so she could understand him. She hoped if he introduced her to his family, that would be like a key and unlock everything. It would explain why he felt uncomfortable among her family, and why he was so fiercely self-reliant.

'May we ride this morning?' she asked. It was cloudy but it was not raining.

'Yes. If you would like to.'

He claimed his family did not care about him, but they must.

'Then I thought we ought to call on your parents before luncheon. I would not wish to call when they may be expecting others. If they do not like me—'

'I did not say they would dislike you, I said they would not be interested in you.' His pitch was cold as he added sugar to his coffee.

'Yet we will go?' she questioned.

His eyebrows lifted as he watched the spoon he spun around in his cup, dissolving the sugar.

She made a face at him, because he was not looking. But he looked up and caught the tail end of her expression.

'Are you sure you want me to take you? I will warn you only once more, it is a bad idea.'

'Yes, I am sure.'

That was not the last time he tried to discourage her. He tried to persuade her against it again on their ride to the park. Then after they'd given the horses their heads for a while and pulled up, he warned her another time; as though he had thought about nothing else for the whole gallop. When he lifted her down from Athena in the stable yard, he pressed her to change her mind and continued trying to dissuade her all the way home. He even ignored the lad who swept the street, who he always spoke to.

His warnings became more adamant as he helped her with her buttons as she took off her habit and put on a day dress.

Then he said repeatedly in the hackney carriage on the way to his parents' town house she would not enjoy this.

Yet in all these warnings not once did he explain why he did not want to take her, beyond saying they would not care that he was married.

She thought they would. She thought she could find out why he was not close to his family and help him fix the problem.

When they reached the town house, which was a tall, wide building in Cavendish Square, Andrew climbed out from the carriage and offered a trembling hand to help her down the step.

This area of London was old money. His family, therefore, had held a place in society for generations. Of course, she could have looked Andrew's family up in *The Peerage* at John's house, the book which indexed the members of titled nobility. But she had not because it would have felt disloyal to research him rather than ask him.

His skin paled as he looked up at the house.

Yesterday he was hesitant when they reached John's – here, he looked afraid.

She wrapped her hand about his arm, it felt as stiff as iron.

He coughed, clearing his throat as though it were dry as they walked to the front door.

I should not have made him come.

The front door opened and the hired carriage pulled away.

It was too late to leave.

As he stepped over the threshold, he became so pale she thought he might be ill.

'Andrew?' she whispered.

'Remember, I warned you,' he said through the side of his mouth, before facing the servant who had opened the door.

'Good morning, Master Drew.'

A stiff-lipped smiled acknowledged the welcome. 'Is the Marquis at home, Mr Potts, and my lady mother?'

She remembered Andrew saying it was the servants who had shortened his name.

'Indeed. Shall I ask if you may be received?'

Mary just managed to stop her jaw dropping. *Why would he need to ask for their permission?*

'That would be the point of me standing here. Please tell the Marchioness, I am here because my wife would like to be introduced.'

'Your wife. Forgive me.' He bowed towards Mary. 'Lady Framlington.' Then he said to Andrew, 'Please wait, I will ask if it is convenient.'

The muscles in Andrew's cheek twitched as the man walked

away and climbed the stairs to the family rooms, leaving them standing in the hall.

Being left in the hall was not odd to him. Nor was it a surprise that the servant had no knowledge of their marriage. That meant if his parents had seen the announcement, they had not discussed it in the house. Servants heard everything.

They stood in silence for five minutes or more before Mr Potts returned.

'The Marchioness will see you.'

They were escorted upstairs to a drawing room, and en route, Andrew established his roguish look of nonchalance.

She could see through this front now – he hid how much he did care behind that swagger.

She would have taken his hand but he held it away from her, over his midriff, giving her the impression he did not want to be touched. He was utterly insular, just as he had been yesterday at John's and during their carriage ride back to London after they'd eloped. Then, as they followed the servant to an open door, she saw his eyes harden with his devil-may-care expression. That look always came before an argument.

'You owe me for this,' Andrew whispered as the servant entered the room ahead of them.

'Lord and Lady Framlington, my lord,' the butler intoned.

'Yes, yes, bring him in,' an impatient woman's voice answered.

Andrew led the way, a pace ahead of Mary.

An older woman with a generous, curvaceous figure, who she presumed to be his mother, sat in a chair near the hearth. She wore a vivid emerald, taffeta morning dress and a matching turban. A stately gentleman with a large, crooked nose sat opposite her, reading a newspaper. Andrew's father, she assumed, although there was no resemblance, either in his face or his build. A tall, slender gentleman, who did have a similar nose to the Marquis, sat on a sofa beside a woman, who was reading a book. Mary noted the wedding ring on her finger. Two younger men lounged in other chairs, sitting sideways, their legs hooked over the arms.

None of them stood to greet her. The men who lounged did not even sit up straight. And none of them acknowledged Andrew.

'Sir.' Andrew bowed even though his father did not look up. 'Mother.' He bowed again. 'I have brought my wife to be introduced to you, at her wish. She did not want to be embarrassed by not knowing you in a public meeting.'

'Potts told us your reason for being here, get on with it,' Andrew's mother said.

Andrew glanced at her, his eyebrows rising. 'Mary, allow me to introduce you to Lord Framlington, the Marquis of Philkins.'

His father looked up, his expression saying he thought Andrew was something abhorrent. He glanced at Mary without comment, then looked back down at the newspaper.

Andrew's Adam's apple slid down and up as he swallowed, it was a nervous gesture.

'And my mother, Lady Framlington.' He looked at his mother.

Mary dropped a deep curtsy, ignoring their lack of interest.

If this was her family, Andrew would have made some silly quip, but he merely progressed. 'My eldest brother, the Earl of Alder, and his wife.' Again, they ignored her as Mary curtsied. 'And my brothers, Lord Jack and Lord Mark.' Mary bobbed a less eloquent curtsy as they stared rudely, still not sitting upright.

The Marquis cleared his throat. 'I cannot see why you have brought this woman here. She is naught to do with me, is she.'

Mary heard Andrew take a deep breath, she imagined him holding in an insulting retort.

It was a mistake to make him bring her here.

'No, sir,' he said. His eyes looked cold and dark with emotions that were fathoms deep. 'However, as we are here, perhaps you could offer Mary tea, Mother?' Belligerence – anger and a false note of arrogance – had slipped into his pitch.

This is where he learned to mask his true emotions.

Warmth spread through Mary's skin, the heat of embarrassment. She had never imagined that he would need to beg for their hospitality. How could she have foreseen this?

'She's a prize beauty,' Jack said to Andrew. 'How the devil did you win her, she's Marlow's, is she not? I suppose she's bloody rich as well, knowing your luck.'

Mary saw a muscle in Andrew's cheek tick.

If one of her brothers had spoken to her like that her father would have reprimanded them, even if they were not children any more.

Her hand wrapped about Andrew's arm. They had not been asked to sit, and his mother had neither confirmed nor denied the offer of refreshment.

'*She* is my wife.' Andrew glared at Jack. 'And therefore Lady Framlington. *She* is also the half-sister of the Duke of Pembroke so if you do not wish to offend the better half of society, mind your words.'

Mary's embarrassment continued as the men stared at her, the Marquis's gaze piercing.

'Edward Marlow would not have given his permission,' the Marquis stated.

Andrew's eldest brother, the Earl of Alder, stood. 'I imagine Drew has been about his usual mischief.'

Mary expected Andrew to reply, but he was silent. His brother walked to a tray of decanters and poured himself a drink. He did not offer Andrew one. He looked at the Marquis. 'Father...'

The desire to get Andrew out of the house pulsed into her limbs. *This is a poisonous place. We should not have come.*

'If you wish for refreshment, Drew, you must tug the bell pull,' his mother said. 'There is no point standing there thinking someone will serve you.'

Mary's cheeks burned on his behalf, but she was not going to let the woman continue to treat her as if she did not exist. She walked across to pull the bell herself.

'She's got a hell of a fine figure on her, ain't she?' Mark said. 'You're a damned lucky basta—'

Mary heard a sudden movement and a strangled sound.

She turned back.

Andrew had gripped the knot of Mark's cravat and twisted the fashionable neck cloth into a noose. 'You will respect my wife. Do you hear me?'

'Drew!' his mother shouted.

The Marquis stood. 'Out!' He pointed at the door. 'You are not welcome here. You never were, and you never will be. You are not my son and I regret the day I let you have my name. Go!'

Andrew thrust his brother back into the chair with a hard shove, let him go, and straightened.

Mary was unsure what to do.

He looked at his mother with scorn, glared defiantly at the Marquis, then held out his hand towards her.

If she could only turn back time, she would hear what he told her and not have brought him here. But how could she have imagined this? What had he done to deserve this? Why had they disowned him?

She took his hand. His fingers closed tightly about hers.

Andrew nodded a scarce bow in the direction of his mother. 'Forgive me for reminding you of my existence.' His voice was cold and condemning.

He turned, pulling Mary in his wake, and they left the room. She looked over her shoulder in the last stride. 'Good day.' His family were not polite, but she had been raised better.

As Andrew's hard footsteps resonated along the hall, his father's voice followed. 'Good riddance!'

The butler encountered them mid-flight. 'Master Drew...'

Andrew cast him a look that was so cold it could have turned him to stone. 'I will show myself out without thieving, Potts. There is nothing I want from this house.'

The butler hurried after them.

'Andrew,' Mary said, in an attempt to slow him down as she struggled to keep up with him. He did not slow. But when they reached the stairs, he released her hand and left her to follow as he jogged down.

If he could have sprouted wings and flown from the house, she thought he would have.

In the hall he opened the door, and left it open for her to follow.

Her heart pounding, she hurried out. He had stopped on the pavement and reached into a pocket of his morning coat. He withdrew a thin cigar and matches. He placed the cigar in his mouth, squatted and struck a match on the pavement, then rose and lit the cigar, drawing heavily on it. He looked upward and blew the smoke out, then looked at her. 'Are you ready then?' His voice sounded emotionless. 'We will walk home, if you do not mind. I cannot smoke in a hansom and it will take several streets to find one anyway, by which time we will be halfway home.'

His arm lifted, offering her the option to lay her hand on his forearm. The action denied what happened only moments ago, as though he did not care.

But he did care. She had seen his anger and she knew him now; she knew that beneath his anger was pain.

She accepted his arm, unsure what to do, and he walked on.

The muscle in his arm beneath her fingers gradually relaxed as he spoke animatedly about the weather, commented on passers-by and carriages, occasionally sucking on his cigar, and then blowing the smoke out away from her.

He had shut what had happened out of his mind in the way a maid might sweep dirt beneath a rug. The memory would still be there to find later.

When arguments exploded among her brothers, her brother Robbie was the quiet one. But he would let disagreements fester. Andrew reminded her of Robbie. *How long has the argument with his family festered?*

If she knew the cause, she could help. Maybe if he apologised, then he and his father could lay new foundations.

As they walked, and he talked nonsense, her mind plotted. Considering ways to help him establish a truce with his family. The argument was hurting him, there must be a way to repair the rift.

When they reached his rooms, she untied the ribbons of her bonnet. 'Why did you fall out with them?' she asked as he closed the door. She pulled the ribbons loose. 'What did you do to upset them?'

'What did I do...' He glared at her.

Her lower lip caught between her teeth for a second, but she wished to speak. She would not be able to stand being at odds with her family. 'I shan't judge you if you tell me, and I might be able to help you heal the rift.'

8

Drew's anger reignited. It had been glowing like coals since they left the Marquis's house. 'The rift... Were you not in the room, Mary?'

Did she need him to spell it out for her? He had no intention of doing so. He was an unwanted bastard. He would not explain that.

'Andrew.' She came towards him, all sweet innocent charm and quiet voice. 'What harm would it do to tell me what happened? Whatever you did it must have been years ago.'

It cut that she automatically laid the blame on him. He thought her opinion of him had changed. That she no longer thought him bad. But this mess was not her fault. He calmed his temper – silencing the urge to yell at her. 'It is not a rift,' he said quietly, walking over to the decanter to pour himself a brandy. 'It is a canyon a mile wide and there are no bridges. Let it rest.'

'But apologies can make—'

'I have nothing to apologise for.' He lifted the stopper from the decanter.

'I know that it often seems that way,' she said more hesitantly, as he half-filled a glass. 'But sometimes an apology can help, even if you do not think you are in the wrong.'

Am I to apologise for my birth?

He swallowed some brandy.

Her fingers slipped about his middle, holding him from behind, as she pressed her cheek against his shoulder. She was offering comfort, but he had a feeling she sought to appease him too.

After a moment, she let go.

He turned.

Her hands hovered in front of her waist, her fingers nervously touching her wedding ring. She looked from the ring to him, her crystal-like eyes looking straight into his eyes. 'Why is your ring inscribed T R? I wondered if it was a family ring, but the initials do not link with anyone.'

Could the woman not work it out for herself? He sipped the brandy.

'I am sorry, I suppose you won it in a game of cards, or...'

Good God. Drew felt his anger soar. *Or?* Was she accusing him of giving her a stolen ring?

'Or what, Mary?' His pitch was low, his temper threatening. 'Say it!' he growled.

She stepped back, grasping the back of a chair to stop herself from falling. 'It is nothing.' Confusion flickered in her beautiful eyes.

But he could not get a grip on his anger. 'Nothing, Mary?' She had unleashed the devil in him. He glared at her. *But damn her!* 'Or that it may be stolen? From whom would I steal it? Why would I give you something of so little meaning? I neither won nor stole your ring.'

'I... I... did n... not m... mean...' she stuttered.

'To assume I must be in the wrong and them right? You meant

every damned word! Well, I am sick of your condemnation. I don't give a damn what you think any more.' He threw the last of the brandy into his mouth, swallowed and turned away from her. 'Think what you damn well wish.' He had to get away.

'Andrew.' She followed him towards the door. 'I just did not understand.'

As he passed the games table, where the chessboard was set for a new game, he turned back, lifting a hand to warn her from coming close. 'I told you I did not want to go there, but you insisted. Are you happy now?'

He felt as though she had pulled a loose thread and he was fraying. 'I have no idea who T R is. But whomever he is, he is my father! Would you have me apologise to the Marquis and my mother, who have always hated that I exist, for her lechery?'

The eyes he had admired so often, and seen strength and humour in, misted with pity.

His anger burned even brighter. 'Do not pity me!'

'Please...' She tried to hold his arm.

He lifted it away. 'Please what? Apologise to them! No!' With that he struck the chess pieces from the board, swiping them onto the floor with the back of his hand, sending them flying with a satisfactory crash, and then for good measure he tipped over the table, so the marble board followed its players.

Then he stormed from the room, his heart racing.

9

Mary paced across the sitting room for the thousandth time. There was no sign of her errant husband.

Her stomach churned with anxiety. It was empty, of course. She had not eaten luncheon, nor dinner, but she hoped to eat supper at the ball they were supposed to be attending.

She looked at the clock, as she had every few minutes. It was nearly ten. She would have to come up with a lie for her father again if Andrew did not take her to the ball. She had changed into her evening dress a long time ago. She managed with the buttons by spinning the dress around, but tying the lacing of her stays was impossible. That garment lay discarded on the bed.

Footsteps ran up the hall stairs. They weren't Andrew's, she knew the sound of his steps.

Where is he?

The footsteps stopped outside their door. A knock hit the wood.

'Drew, old devil, are you in?' It was Lord Brooke. 'You are forever closeted away with that wife of yours, and your old friend needs you.'

Mary had assumed Andrew was with his friends, so, if Lord Brooke was here, where was Andrew?

She opened the door, a blush heating her cheeks. 'L-L-Lord Brooke. A-A-Andrew is not at home. I thought he was with you.'

'I have not seen him for a couple of days. May I wait for him?' He walked past her, without waiting for her invitation, and headed to Andrew's brandy decanter.

'I do not know how long he will be. He had to go out unexpectedly.' Uncertain what to do, she closed the door. She had never been alone in a room with any man other than her family or Andrew.

He helped himself to a drink. 'No matter.' He turned. 'As you have dressed for the evening, I assume you do expect him back.'

'I thought I would dress in case, but I am not sure... We were meeting my parents at a ball.' Mary kept her distance, her fingers on the door handle behind her back.

His dark brown eyes danced with humour as he drank from the glass. 'But he has left you at home, a damsel in distress.' He smiled, but the smile fell when he caught sight of the chessboard.

Mary had righted the table, placed the board back on it and reset the pieces, but the board was broken in two.

'Where were you going?' he asked.

'To the Caldecotts'.'

He smiled, drank the rest of the brandy and put the glass down. 'Lady Framlington, as Drew's friend I believe it is my duty, and it shall also be my pleasure, to see you safely to the Caldecotts' ball. If you will allow it?' He bowed briefly, but not insultingly.

Her mind whirled in a turmoil. If she went with Lord Brooke her father would be less likely to think something was amiss. But what about Andrew? He knew they had agreed to meet her parents – he would know where to find her.

'Yes, thank you, Lord Brooke, I would appreciate your escort, if it will not disrupt your night.'

'It will not. My carriage is here, so it will not take long to reach the Caldecotts'.'

'I will fetch my cloak.' She hurried into the bedchamber, her heartbeat thumping.

Her cloak hung over one of her trunks. She picked it up and turn—

Lord Brooke stood at the bedchamber door. 'Let me,' he said, entering and taking the cloak from her hands.

She turned so he could lay it on her shoulders.

She secured the buttons at the front, her fingers shaking.

Perhaps it was madness accepting Lord Brooke's escort, a man she only knew by his awful reputation. Yet he was Andrew's friend and she trusted Andrew's judgement. A lesson she wished she had recognised this morning when he told her she would not want to meet his parents.

When she faced Lord Brooke, she was met with a broad, roguish grin. Her heart lurched as the smile reminded her of Andrew's brazen expressions.

Where is he? Should I wait? He could be ten minutes from home, or playing cards somewhere with no intent to return. Waiting here would make her more maudlin and her father angrier. No, it was better she went and shielded him from her father's response to his absence. After all, he had left her here, so he could hardly complain about her going.

Lord Brooke offered his arm. She nervously laid her fingers on it. 'Thank you, Lord Brooke.'

'Call me Peter, my dear, if we are to be friends, which I hope we are.' He patted her hand.

She smiled. 'Call me Mary then.'

During the carriage ride to the Caldecotts', he kept talking, flirting, but not in a threatening way; as though he realised she was nervous being in a confined space with him.

Outside the Caldecotts' house, the carriage rocked as Lord Brooke's groom jumped from the perch at the rear. The door opened.

Lord Brooke descended then took her hand and helped her.

Her fingers shook furiously when she queued to be acknowledged by the receiving line.

'Lady Framlington and Lord Brooke,' the footman informed Lady Caldecott.

Lady Caldecott's eyes shone with unspoken questions as Mary curtsied and Peter bowed. Mary bobbed another curtsy to Lord Caldecott, then she was past them and walking the few yards to reach her parents.

Mary's gaze focused on her father. He saw her and frowned as she approached.

'Papa,' she said immediately, pre-empting his questions. 'Andrew was not able to come; something urgent arose. Lord Brooke kindly offered to escort me instead.' Mary looked back at Lord Brooke. 'Thank you, Peter, it was very kind of you to volunteer.'

He bowed graciously, and she hoped, ungraciously, he would go away.

Her father's eyebrows lifted in criticism of Lord Brooke.

The orchestra struck up the tune of a waltz. Instantly Peter bowed. 'Mary, my dear, would you do me the honour?'

Nausea tumbled through Mary's stomach. He was being gallant but she did not want to dance. Yet, if she refused, her father would think she felt unsafe with Lord Brooke.

'Thank you.' She accepted Lord Brooke's hand, without even having said *good evening* to her mother. It did not feel right.

His hand closed around hers, and he embraced her, as

couples began to circle the floor. It felt too intimate. She had not even danced a waltz with Andrew...

10

Just past ten o'clock, Drew ran upstairs in The Albany. He had been walking off his irritation for hours and now he was late for the ball. He bore no anger towards Mary, she was not responsible for his birth. But today's experience had humiliated him and re-opened childhood wounds.

It was not until a church clock struck nine times that he realised how late it had become. He had rushed back, cursing himself for deserting her again.

The handle turned but the door did not open. It was locked. Mary must have given up on him and gone to bed – at least that was what he hoped.

He unlocked the door and went in.

She was not in the parlour. Guilt grasping in his gut, he checked the bedchamber. She was not there either, but her items were, including the stays she was unable to secure herself that had been left on the bed. She had not left him, then.

In the parlour, the chessboard was back on the table, but it was broken in two. He noticed two used glasses standing with the decanters. The one he had drunk from before leaving, the other she must have used...

He felt as cold as stone. *Where is she?*

With her family, common sense replied. She would have sent word to her father and they would have collected her. She must be at the ball, and he could meet her there.

The smell of her perfume hovered in his rooms as he put on his evening dress. Arriving late was better than not arriving at all.

He reached the Caldecotts' house in less than thirty minutes. The receiving line had broken up and the ballroom was full. His spine stiffened as he joined the crush, preparing to face her father.

The light from a few hundred candles shimmered in the glass of chandeliers and glittered from the mirrors lining the hall. The same mirrors reflected London society in all its splendour. Marlow and Pembroke were easy to spot. Like him, they were a head above most of the women and some of the men. Drawn like metal to a loadstone, his spirit cried for Mary as he made his way through the crowd. But still he could not see her.

He stopped, his gaze skimming over the dark heads of hair among those dancing. *There*, the exact shade of ebony secured in a high knot by a silver comb that had lain on his dresser earlier today.

His feet became as heavy as lead as his blood turned to ice, and a red mist clouded his vision. She was waltzing with Peter! *What the hell?*

Peter's hand rested on her slender back, and his other held hers, leading her through the dance.

She had not used the second glass in his room; Peter had been in his rooms with her. And now here!

The thread that had come loose this morning unravelled at a rate of knots as his hands balled into fists. He did not hear music, nor conversation. No one existed but him and the two of them as he walked among the dancers. People stumbled, bumped into him and complained as they pulled their partners out of his way.

The music finished with a flourish and couples separated.

Peter's hands fell and Mary stepped back smiling, the colour in her cheeks high and her eyes bright.

Drew's stride lengthened.

Mary looked his way and her mouth opened.

Peter turned too.

Then Drew reached them.

He thumped Peter's shoulder with his left hand, knocking him away from Mary. Peter stumbled back a step. Then Drew thrust his right fist at Peter's jaw. The impact satisfyingly reverberated up Drew's arm as Peter lost his balance and fell on his arse.

A chorus of screams rang out, along with deeper notes of masculine disapproval.

Peter would have risen, but Drew struck his shoulder with the heel of his shoe, keeping him sprawled on the floor. 'Traitor!' The word echoed about the high ceiling.

'Andrew! Please stop!' Mary's hand held onto his right arm.

Peter leaned up on one elbow.

Drew was not done. He pulled his arm away from Mary and dropped to one knee. 'Leave my wife alone. Do you hear?' He would have grasped Peter's neckcloth but Peter caught his wrist.

'I was doing you a favour,' Peter growled, his voice containing disgust.

'I don't care. Don't touch her. Do you understand?'

'I only danced with her.'

'Do you understand?'

'For God's sake, don't be ridiculous. You are making fools of us both,' Peter snarled.

Drew clasped Peter's cravat and twisted it as his other knee came down on Peter's chest.

'Enough!' a domineering yell rang out, as someone grabbed the collar at the back of Drew's evening coat and pulled him back. Drew released Peter with a shove as he was pulled to his feet. 'You are embarrassing my daughter,' Marlow hissed into Drew's ear. Then, 'The show is over,' he said in a loud voice to those watching, releasing Drew's collar.

The Duke of Arundel helped Peter to his feet.

Mary's skin was pallid, and one hand hovered over her stomach as though she were nauseous.

Hell. He had done it now; he could not be a good enough man for her.

But Drew's whole being revolted at the thought of Peter's hands on her, of him in a room alone with her.

'I will call for our carriage,' her father said.

'We are going now, anyway.' Drew looked at Mary and held out his hand.

She did nothing.

He raised his hand higher, saying come to me, and desperately hoped she would...

Her hand slotted into his, in that perfect fit he had become accustomed to. But a vicelike pain clenched about his heart as he remembered her hand in Peter's moments ago.

He turned away from Peter and her family, taking her with him. He would not apologise for who he was. *They can like me or not. I do not care.*

All his life that spiteful voice inside him would have then shouted, *I only care for my friends. So, what now...?*

So what if I no longer have Peter? I have Harry and Mark. And he had Mary. She could not leave him.

Drew forced a path through the crowd, pulling Mary by the hand behind him.

In the hall, he told a footman to find her cloak quickly. That was where her parents caught up with them.

'Lord Framlington!' Marlow's strides ate up the last few yards.

Mary's loyalty was to be tested in another tug of war.

'What did you think you were doing? People are gossiping.'

'What do I care?' Drew snarled.

'I care,' Marlow answered, his voice low and threatening. 'And Mary cares. You will have her ostracised. You are hurting my daughter.'

'Mary, come home with us.' Marlow's voice became soft and understanding. 'We should not have let this happen. This is enough. We will protect you.'

From what? *From me!*

The wind blew out from the sails of Drew's anger. This was another moment of choice: her family or him. Drew's jaw locked hard.

Her hand held his more firmly. 'No, Papa, Andrew and I are going home. Do not worry. I will call at John's tomorrow.'

Relief raced beneath his skin, as cold as ice, through blood and bone and sinew. But it was too late for her to cling to him now, she had torn his heart in two. He had turned to stone inside.

Her father sighed.

'My lady.' A footman brought Mary's cloak.

Her mother took it and lay it on Mary's shoulders, while Drew held her hand as though he were drowning in a swelling sea and Mary was driftwood. The pain from his rib, he realised now as it was no longer masked by anger, was excruciating. He could barely breathe as they turned to the door.

'Tomorrow...' her father said, as though he would try to persuade her to leave again tomorrow.

Drew knew, now, she would not leave. She would be like his mother, stay for the sake of appearances when there was no love – and be unfaithful. He was not good enough – he was not lovable. She would turn to other men for love, men who were more like the members of her family, like Peter, and Drew would go mad with jealousy.

A shiver ran up his spine as they walked along the street.

A hansom carriage waited on a far corner. Drew raised his hand, beckoning to the driver. 'The Albany,' he called up their destination and opened the door for Mary.

11

The carriage rumbled, creaked and bounced over uneven cobbles, the horses' iron shoes ringing on the London stone.

Mary couldn't think of anything to say. Her husband had stormed out of their rooms, then stormed into the Caldecotts' ballroom with the force of a hurricane. Now it felt as though she were sitting in the eye of the storm. He had neither spoken nor moved since he sat beside her. He sat with the ankle of one leg resting on the other knee, his elbow on the shallow ledge of the carriage window, and he looked out, his eyes focusing on nothing.

Rain began striking the window and the carriage roof in a hard pitter-patter. She looked at the drops of rain landing on the pane of glass on her side.

She should never have made him go to his parents. This was not anger, it was pain. She had wanted to understand all of him, and, oh, how she understood now. He said in the beginning that he did not know what love was. No, he had never been loved, nor loved, until she fell in love with him and he fell in love with her.

Then she had called him a liar...

She sighed.

He turned his head and his gaze towards her.

His observation made her skin tingle, but she did not look back at him.

The first time she met him, she saw the dangerous secrets in his eyes. But now she could see through him, she knew he had been longing, and hoping, to be welcomed and liked. When he was afraid of rejection, he was at his most dangerous.

'*Don't pity me!*' Those had been his last words before he left this afternoon.

She did not want to pity him, she just wanted to love him – and to be loved by him. But the silence between them was a wall she had no idea how to scale. His pain was a fortress. All she could do was wait for his defences to fall again.

The silence continued when they reached The Albany and climbed the stairs to their rooms. When he closed the apartment door, she told him, 'I will retire,' and went into the bedchamber.

He followed. 'I will undo the buttons at your back.'

'Thank you.'

When the buttons were freed, he left the room.

She heard him pour a drink in the sitting room, as she undressed and changed into her nightdress.

A sharp sound of glass shattering against the stone hearth, made every muscle in her body jump. She knew him now, she knew he had broken the glass Peter drank from.

She climbed into bed, her stomach growling with hunger. She had not eaten but she was not hungry. Nor could she sleep. She lay facing the door. It stood ajar. She could see a candle burning and hear him pacing.

When he came to bed a long while later, he undressed in the dark. The mattress rocked as he lay down, but he did not touch her. It felt as if he were deliberately trying to keep his distance.

12
___

She woke to the smell of fried bacon, fresh bread, coffee and chocolate, and opened her eyes as her stomach rumbled loudly. She felt sick with hunger as she pushed the covers back and got up.

In the parlour, Andrew sat in an armchair, with a newspaper open on his lap. One place at the table had a plate with crumbs on it and a cup that was stained with coffee grounds.

'Good morning,' she ventured.

He did not look up from the newspaper. 'I have ordered breakfast, luncheon and dinner for each day as you will not order for yourself. If you are not here, anything uneaten I will give to the street boys. I am going to Tattersall's today to buy a carriage and a pair of horses to pull it. I will employ a driver at the stables. It will be yours, Mary. You may then go wherever you like, whenever you please.'

'So I will have no need of an escort...?'

'Quite so.' His voice was bitter. He was still angry. Still full of pain.

Mary sat at the table. She had no idea how to respond.

'I will also employ a lady's maid to come in the morning and evening, to help you dress.'

'And to undress?' Mary's voice had become quiet with uncertainty. *Is he saying he will have nothing more to do with me?*

'She will await your return.'

Mary stood again, her hand closing about the top of the chair as her legs felt weak. 'Peter only took me to the ball because you were not here.'

He stood too, folded the newspaper and tossed it on top of the broken chessboard. 'I am going riding.'

'If you wait, I will dress and come with you.'

Lacklustre hazel eyes looked back at her. 'That is not necessary.'

'Not necessary... Do you not want me to be with you?'

He turned away. 'You will have your carriage by tomorrow, you may go to your brother's and ride his horses then. Or Peter has some good ones, I am sure he would oblige.'

'Do not be ridiculous! Spite does not suit you. It was one waltz!' she yelled at his back.

He looked at her now. 'We both know I am not good enough for you, so why delay the inevitable? You will find someone else. I am going out.'

'Andrew, stop. You cannot shut me out of your life over one waltz.' She followed him to the door, where he lifted his long riding coat from a peg.

'That is not the issue.' He picked up his gloves.

'I know the issue is your family. It is not me.'

His gaze met hers. His dark eyes desolate.

'Andrew.' Her fingers touched the fading bruises on his cheek.

'Let me go, Mary.'

'To where?'

'*I am going riding.* I will come back at midday and take you to your parents and then go to Tat's to find you a carriage and horses.'

Tears burned in Mary's eyes. 'You can be cruel.'

'Me cruel? You insisted I introduce you to my parents, and you accepted Peter's escort.'

'And they are sins?'

'It does not matter. Just let me go. I do not wish to argue with you.'

'Andrew...' It felt as though he was leaving her.

He stared at her, his hat and gloves in his hands and his coat over his arm.

Mary's hands dropped to her sides, and she nodded. There was no point in arguing, he was unreachable in this mood.

13

When Drew returned from his ride, a large carriage was standing outside The Albany. Pembroke's coat of arms was emblazoned on the side, and its brass trim shone in the sunshine. It had been there a while because two grooms in the Pembroke livery held the heads of four glossy black horses.

What did Pembroke want? Drew's patience was paper-thin. One wrong word would be all it took and he would slam Pembroke up against a wall.

Drew entered the apartment without knocking; these were *his* rooms. But Pembroke was not there. Mary, her mother and an aunt, the Duchess of Wiltshire, looked at him.

They had sent the women to do battle again.

It was extremely early to be calling. They must be trying to find out how well he kept her.

He looked at the table. A second used plate stood beside the remains of their breakfast. At least Mary had eaten. He may be angry with her and wish to hold her at arm's length, but he still cared and she would make herself ill if she did not eat.

He lifted his hat and bowed to the women.

Lady Marlow stood. 'Good morning, Lord Framlington. I am glad you returned, we thought we might miss you. We came to invite Mary to accompany us to the Duchess of Bradford's garden party this afternoon.'

Her aunt stood too. 'I am on my way to Margaret's and thought it would be nice to call in rather than send a message.'

What nonsense! Mary's cousin lived streets away and Drew's apartment was not en route. They had come to spy.

Drew looked at Mary, wondering what she had told them. *That I am an ignorant monster, probably; incapable of loving her and unable to be loved.*

But he was not cowed. Mary may not have extravagance and excess here, but she had everything she needed – if she chose to ask for it, that was. Joseph told him this morning that Mary had eaten neither luncheon nor dinner the day before. That was when he had decided to take control of everything. The decision also eased his conscience. Employing servants to care for her meant he could withdraw without fear or guilt.

'Does my home live up to your expectations, Lady Marlow?' he asked.

'It is not my expectations that matter, is it?' Her answer was shrewish.

'No, it is Mary's, and she has everything she needs,' he said. *Except a man she can love.*

'Except a husband who can apply restraint, Lord Framlington.'

'Mama.' Mary stood, but not in defence of her mother. She walked across the room and stood beside him. As though he might care what her mother thought. But it made it obvious that Mary had not told them the man she married was a hell-born bastard.

'Your mother is right,' her aunt said. 'Your behaviour last night, Lord Framlington, was unforgivable.'

Mary's chin lifted.

Drew sighed. He did not want her to argue with her family on his behalf. The time for that had passed. She needed her family, not him. 'You're quite right, Your Grace, Lady Marlow. I am sorry I spoiled the evening, but it is water under the bridge today, and as you can see, I do not feed Mary gruel or lock her up, so you may report back that all is well here.'

Both women stared at him, their pale-blue eyes the spit of Mary's. With the same ability to freeze a man with an icy cool glare.

'You are not amusing,' her mother stated.

'Yes, you told me that before, Lady Marlow. I shall try to remember in future that you do not appreciate my humour.'

Mary held his arm, warning him to be kind.

'Should we call for you after luncheon, Mary?' her aunt asked.

'I will deliver her,' he said. Her aunt's and mother's eyebrows rose. 'Have no fear, I will not stay. I imagine I am not invited.'

'I will meet you there,' Mary said.

The women stood still, as if they were afraid to leave her here. He would let them stay longer.

'Did you call for tea, Mary?' He looked at her, then he could not stop his devil speaking to her mother. 'Or I can offer you a brandy to help you suffer my company.'

'There is no need for spite,' the Duchess of Arundel stated.

'My sentiments exactly,' he replied.

Mary's fingernails dug into the fabric of his coat.

'Very well, ladies, as I am unwelcome here, I shall withdraw and leave you with Mary. Your servant.' He bowed to one then the other as Mary's fingers slipped from his arm, and a moment later he walked back downstairs, with nowhere to go. It was too early to go to Tattersall's. He went to the stables, spoke to his horses and told the grooms to prepare the phaeton for the time he needed it. Then leaning against one side of the entrance arch, he smoked a thin cigar as he watched the front door of The Albany, waiting for the women to leave.

A smile pulled at one side of his lips as he noticed the little street sweep, Timmy, hovering around the horses. The boy had smelt the wealth in the air, probably in the wax polish on the shining coach.

It was not long before they came out.

'Can I open the door for you, ma'am?' he heard Timmy say, even though the women had footmen.

He could not see the women ascend from this side, but he heard the door close, and then Timmy walked around the corner staring at a coin in his hand.

It made Drew feel as though he was even lower in Lady Marlow's esteem than a street sweep.

I do not care!

The carriage rolled away, and he crossed the street, taking an opportunity to knock Timmy's hat off. 'You don't need my pennies today, lad.'

The boy laughed.

When he entered the parlour, Mary was seated in an armchair, with a small pile of letters in her lap, one of them open in her hand. She looked up. 'Mama brought my post.'

'Who are they from?'

'My cousins, and this...' she held up the letter she had just opened, 'is from my younger brother Robbie.' Her concentration returned to the letter and her face lit up as she read.

It was impossible not to love her. But he had to stop, because he could not bear it when the time came that she would succumb to a better man.

Drew put his hat and gloves down, took off his riding coat and hung it on a peg. Then walked over to collect the newspaper that had been left in the other armchair. He sat down and opened it at the page he had been reading, only to realise Mary had stopped reading the letter and was reading him.

She looked extremely pretty in the dusky pink muslin dress she had chosen to wear today. The dress had embroidered rose buds at the hems of her sleeves and skirt.

'You did not have to be rude to my mother.'

'She came here to spy.'

'She came to see if I was well. Which I was, until yesterday.'

Until she met his parents and discovered he was a worthless bastard. He would not wish to be married to himself. He shrugged and raised the open newspaper, deliberately covering his face.

'And now you hide from me.'

Coward. 'Persist and I will go out,' he responded from behind the newspaper.

'Again?'

'If I wish to, yes. I can do as I please, as can you.'

He heard the fabric of her dress stirring as she stood, and her light footsteps, then the newspaper was crushed down. Her blue eyes flashed fire. 'So, is this it? You will not even claim to love me anymore.'

Oh, I love you, but I know your love will wither and die. Because I was wrong. We are not made for one another.

Her hands settled on her hips. His little firecracker. *Not mine, some other man's.* It hurt to think it, but he must.

'I love you,' she said angrily.

'You have no business doing so.' He schooled his gaze, closing the shutters on his emotions. 'Your family have it right, Mary. I am sorry I disappointed you.'

'And you discovered this yesterday…?'

God, the woman could be clever. 'I discovered it last night.'

'Because I let your friend, who you told me I should trust, escort me to a ball in your stead and dance with me.'

He folded the newspaper and threw it aside, standing as he did so. She stepped back. 'I *was* only ever pretending, and as you are determined to pursue an argument, I will go out.' He walked around her, picked up his hat and put it back on his head.

'You have a letter too. Joseph brought it up,' she said as he pulled on his gloves.

The folded letter struck his sleeve and fell onto the floorboards.

He squatted down and picked it up. It was from Caro. His younger sister's hasty handwriting formed his name in sharp strokes. It had no seal because she would want the letter to remain private. He took the letter with him as he left and stopped to read it in the street. She was confined to her bed. Kilbride had beaten her severely and she had lost a third child.

Drew was never sure which came first, the beating or the loss of a child.

He sighed. It had to end either way. He was unable to help himself, but he could help Caro. He would organise somewhere for her to run to, where she could live anonymously.

14

Two weeks later, Drew wandered down an aisle in the House of Millard, a warehouse in Cheapside, which sold Bengal muslins and flannels. Caro hung onto his arm. Despite the obscurity of their meeting place, she wore a fine gauze veil, perhaps to hide the bruises.

Kilbride had banned her from consorting with her rakehell brother. But when Caro asked to see him, Drew planned clandestine ways to meet her.

As the two illegitimate children, both excluded and ill-treated in their childhood, they had become each other's sanctuary.

When she reached the age of sixteen, the Marquis sold Caro to the highest bidder on the marriage market, disposing of his second embarrassment. She was ostracised like Drew. None of their family acknowledged her in public or private, and she had no friends because Kilbride forbade her to have any contact with others.

She was in the room the night he hit Peter. So was their mother and the Marquis. He hated that they must have seen how much his visit dislodged his self-control, or rather his self-worth.

Now he had no family, wife or friends; none of his friends had contacted him.

Pain tightened around his chest, holding firm, like an invisible metal band. This pain had haunted him ever since that night.

'I have found a house for you,' he said to Caro.

'I cannot leave him, Drew.'

Drew sucked in a breath, trying to dispel the tension in his chest. 'If you do not leave, he will kill you eventually. The place I have found is a small cottage in Maidstone, not far from London, so I may visit frequently. I will employ a woman to manage it, cook and clean and such.'

'What if he finds me?'

'Why should he? He has no reason to go to Maidstone and you may change your name.'

They stopped talking as two women walked past them.

'You will not be able to take much with you, though—'

'I cannot leave.'

He stopped and faced her. 'If you do not then I will challenge Kilbride to a duel and either I will be shot dead or go to prison for shooting him. Then where will we be?'

She lowered her head.

She was a tiny, slender woman, fragile but not weak. He had always admired her bravery. She never complained, merely coped. But they had learned stamina and endurance as children.

His palm rested on her shoulder. 'Will you give me a date?'

She lifted her head. 'I shall send word when I can.'

He took her hand and squeezed it gently.

'And you? I have not even asked how you are. How is your wife?'

'Miserable.' A roguish grin caught at his lips, though it was not amusing.

'*You are not amusing, Lord Framlington.*' No. I am human wreckage and I must either laugh or... kill myself.

He shrugged. 'The poor girl married me, and I am a bitter, twisted bastard. As you know.'

Her arms lifted and she hugged him briefly. 'You are not. Do not spoil what you have.'

'Too late, I am afraid. You were at the Caldecotts' so you saw.'

'She is nice, Drew, and kind—'

'Which is exactly why I will never fit with her.'

'If you do not intend to try, you should not have married her.'

'I know that now. But the deed is done, she has paid my debts and she will find happiness in some other way.'

'You will leave her?' She sounded horrified.

He sighed. He had thought about it, but he could not do it, not yet. He needed more time. More time to set her in his memory and keep her there. He forced a smile, giving Caro no answer.

'Do not leave her. She is good for you.'

'No. Mary is bad for me, and I am very bad for her. She makes me lose control.' *She makes me face who I am, and I hate myself because I care what she thinks.*

'Have you apologised to Peter?'

'I have not seen Peter.'

'Drew, do not destroy your life.' Her fingers touched the fading bruises around his cheek and eye. 'Bruises heal. Even the inner ones.'

'You had better go, Caro. You are wasting time worrying over me, save your concern for yourself. Contact me when you know you will have time to get away, and promise me you will not renege.'

'I promise,' she said quietly, committing herself. He had waited years to hear her agree to flee that monster.

She pressed a kiss on his cheek, through the layer of gauze, then left him.

Drew turned in the opposite direction and saw the two women in a far aisle. One was touching the fabrics, the other had been looking their way.

There was something familiar about her, but she too was wearing a fashionable veil on her bonnet, a sweep of white that covered the upper part of her face, and her eyes.

Even if they knew him, though, Caro's black veil had covered her whole face, tucking beneath her chin, and the fabric was so heavy he doubted they could have recognised her.

15

Jennifer leaned closer, holding out her embroidery work. 'Mary, show me how to do this stitch again...'

'She is reading to me,' Jemima complained.

'I can do both.' Mary took the cloth and sewed one stitch, explaining it, then passed the linen square back and recommenced the story.

She had a headache. She rubbed her temple with her fingertips. The headache had become a frequent complaint since Andrew had withdrawn from her.

He had been true to his word; she had a carriage, a driver and groom, a lady's maid who came in daily and a husband who did not love her. He hardly spoke to her and never touched her, and when he could find a reason not to be at home he avoided her.

She spent her days and evenings with her parents, living much as she had before they wed, apart from returning to The Albany to change into her evening clothes, and to sleep in Drew's bed, even though he did not sleep there. He slept in a chair in the parlour.

She had no idea how he filled his days and evenings.

At the end of each day her father would walk her up to the door of Andrew's rooms. She would unlock the door, not knowing if Andrew was there. Her father waited until she shut the door behind her and he heard it lock before he left.

When Andrew was in his rooms, he would not talk but she did. Sprouting a continual inane chatter about everything and anything that happened to avoid the silence. Conversely, she never spoke of Andrew to her family. But nor did they ask after him.

When she began calling earlier and lengthening her stays, she told her father Andrew was busy finding a property for them. She did not even know if he still intended to move. Her father had not asked about Andrew's absence since, apparently simply content that he was not with her.

She was everything but content. Her heart was shattered and she had been tired and listless for days as well as nauseous. She could neither eat nor sleep. She came to John's to fill her days, but she had no desire for anyone's company. A large group of her aunts, uncles and cousins were downstairs, so Mary had come up to the nursery with the girls.

'Mary.'

She jumped. Her Aunt Jane stood behind her. Jemima was startled awake, she had fallen asleep on Mary's lap.

Aunt Jane pressed a palm on Mary's shoulder. 'There is something I need to tell you.' She lifted Jemima into her arms. 'Come along, darling, you are sleepy, you need a nap.' She looked at one of the nursery maids. 'Please put Miss Jemima to bed.' She passed Jemima over, then looked at the other girls. 'There is tea and cake being served downstairs.'

The girls left their embroidery and games, and hurried from the room, sounding more like stampeding elephants than young ladies.

Wariness crept up Mary's spine as her aunt sat on the sofa beside her, her expression a picture of concern. 'Please leave us,' she told the maids who had begun tidying up after the girls. Her eyes followed the maids until the door closed behind them. Then she looked at Mary.

Mary put Jemima's book down on the cushion between them.

'I wish I did not have to tell you this,' her aunt said quietly. 'I have known for a few days but I have been warring with myself over whether or not to speak. Yet, I would never forgive myself if you heard it from someone else.'

Butterflies took flight in her stomach, a million of them. It could not be good news, and it must be about Andrew.

Aunt Jane reached forward and held Mary's left hand in both of hers. 'Mary, there is no easy way to say this...'

How worse could things get?

'A good friend of mine, Violet, Lady Sparks, who you know and would trust as well as I, saw Lord Framlington with a young woman. She was wearing a veil, to hide her identity, but Violet said they looked... affectionate. Violet is not a gossip, you know. She has only told me because she is concerned. We have told no one else, not even your Uncle Robert because he would say something to your father.

'Violet was with her sister-in-law who she believes did not recognise Lord Framlington. I am sorry, because Violet thought, well...' Aunt Jane's eyebrows lifted, communicating what she found it too uncomfortable to say.

'He has a mistress.' Mary had not considered it since he said he could not afford one. Her whole body became numb. She thought the distance between them was her fault, because she made him speak to his family and accepted Lord Brooke's escort.

Her hand felt cold in Aunt Jane's warm hands.

'They were in a draper's, so, it is very likely she is his

mistress. If the gossips find out they will dine on the news because many people in society hold a grievance with Lord Framlington.'

Mary wanted to press her palms over her ears. She shook her head. He said he could not afford a mistress but now he had her dowry.

He loved me for less than one month.

'It is up to you what you do, of course it is, and there is no definite evidence she is his mistress. But if you stay with him and the rumours begin, it will be unpleasant in the least. You will not be welcomed anywhere, even though you have done nothing wrong.'

'You think I should leave him.'

'It is your choice. But you are not happy. We all see it. You barely spend an hour at his rooms. There is no shame in leaving. The whole family will protect you. Perhaps your father, or Robert, or John, could have him followed so you would have evidence and grounds to sue for a divorce.'

It is not that simple.

'I need to think,' she said, withdrawing her hand from her aunt's. 'Please do not tell anyone.'

Jane's smile was warm and sympathetic.

'Don't pity me!' Andrew yelled in her head. She understood that anger.

Her entire family pitied her. Everyone looked at her with sadness in their eyes.

But she would not pity herself. She had made this choice.

'Aunt Jane, would you take me home? My carriage driver is not due to return until after three.'

'Will he be there?'

'I doubt it.' At least now she knew where Andrew went.

'Will you leave him today?'

'No. I need to think.' What could she do when she loved him so much?

'My dear.' Aunt Jane's arms rose, offering an embrace, but Mary sat rigidly straight. 'I was separated from your uncle for years, but we found each other again. Fate will always run its course. There is someone who will love you as you deserve.'

'But I love Andrew. I do not want anyone else. Please take me home. I could not sit among everyone downstairs today.'

'Of course I will.'

'I shall say goodbye to Mama, or she will know something is wrong.'

* * *

The door of Andrew's apartment was locked. He was not there. She was glad, because Aunt Jane had insisted on coming to the rooms with her. She opened the door and encouraged Aunt Jane to come in. The luncheon that had been delivered stood untouched on the table.

Aunt Jane looked about the small sitting room. 'Your mother told me he joked that he keeps you locked up.'

'He likes to annoy Mama and Papa.'

Jane sighed. 'Would you like me to stay awhile?'

'He really does not chain me up, Aunt Jane.'

'But nor does he make you smile.'

Mary noticed her aunt looking at the broken chessboard, her gaze lingering as she pondered the cause of it.

'Things were good between us,' Mary told her. 'Until the day of the Caldecotts' ball. It is my fault everything changed. I insisted on meeting his parents. He did not want to take me. He said they would not want to see him or me, but I persuaded him. He was right, of course. He knows his own family.'

'I think it humiliated him to be treated so horribly in front of me. That is when he broke the chessboard, just in case you think he threw it at me; he did not. He tipped it over in anger, went out and was not back in time for the ball.

'His friend, Lord Brooke, called and offered to take me. That too was a nail in the coffin. He has not forgiven me for allowing Lord Brooke to escort me. But Andrew is polite. He is not ill-treating me. I have everything I need. My meals are provided, I have a maid and a carriage. And we do not share the bed any more. He will not touch me, and he does not spend time with me...' Pain sliced through her heart.

'And now there is another woman, and I suppose it never really was good.' Mary crumpled into a chair and pressed a palm to her forehead as her headache throbbed.

She had forced herself to smile through the goodbyes at John's. She did not have the strength to smile any more.

Her aunt touched her shoulder. 'My first marriage was not good; it was arranged and I had no family to turn to. I had to endure it; you do not. Do not spend your life tied up in a mistake. Walk away, with your head high. You can live with Uncle Robert and I in Yorkshire if you want to escape. He would not mind, you know he would not.'

'What is this? A witches' coven—'

Mary looked up. She had not heard Andrew open the door.

'But there are only two of you. You need three to turn me into a toad.' He pulled his gloves off. 'I presume, *I* am the mistake.' He held his gloves in a fisted hand as he stared at Mary. 'Are you leaving me then?' Accusation strengthened his pitch.

'Lord Framlington.' Aunt Jane stepped into battle.

Mary did not move. Let him rant, he was in the wrong, he had another woman.

'If Mary leaves you, it is because you deserve it. You selfish, heartless man.'

His lips pinched together. At least he was trying to restrain his anger.

'My niece is loved by her family! We will not let her suffer like this!'

Mary stood. This was enough, her head hurt too much to listen to them argue.

Andrew looked from her aunt to her, and the fight seemed to suddenly drop out of him. His shoulders and expression shifted from tense to slack.

'I know you have—' her aunt yelled.

Mary grasped her arm. 'Aunt Jane, thank you for bringing me home. I will speak to you tomorrow.' If anyone confronted him about his mistress it would be her, not her aunt.

'If you are sure?' She was flushed with anger and indignation.

'I am.' Mary's voice held little conviction, her head hurt too much.

Andrew stepped out of the way so she could show Aunt Jane out. They kissed each other's cheeks.

'Goodbye,' Mary said.

'Good day, Lady Barrington,' Andrew said, behind her. 'It was good of you to call and beg my wife to leave me.'

Mary closed the door as her aunt walked away.

'So, are you?' Andrew faced her.

'I hate you when you are like this.' Mary said, ignoring the question and seeking the peace and silence of the bedchamber.

'You are then... You are leaving me.' He followed.

'It is probably what you hope for.' Her speech slurred as her vision became a screen of shifting coloured zigzag patterns. Her hand gripped the doorframe as they blinded her.

'Hope for...' He sounded confused.

'You have pushed me away from the moment we wed.' Her arm stretched out, her hand searching through the colours as she tried to reach the bed that she could not see, nausea rolling in her stomach. She felt hot, then cold and clammy. If she could just reach the bed and lie down.

'Do they still think I was after your money?'

'Were you not?' Bitterness soured her voice as her fingertips found the bedpost. But it was too late. 'I do not feel well. Andrew, I am going to vomit.'

The room tilted, lurching sideways, and everything went black. She hit the floor heavily and the contents of her stomach spewed from her throat.

The next thing she knew she was lying on the soft mattress not the floor, with the cool porcelain of a chamber pot on the bed beside her. But the zigzag colours were still dancing. 'I cannot see,' she sobbed, and then she retched and the pot was pressed closer so she could be sick into it.

She was horribly sick, before this man who had lied to her and did not care about her. She could not be more humiliated.

He gave her a towel. She wiped her mouth, holding on to it as he moved the chamber pot. 'I will wash this out.' He must have cleaned the floor too.

She lay down and closed her eyes, longing for sleep, to escape the pain. Tears rolled across her lashes and ran down her cheeks. She curled up her knees, wrapping herself up small like a dormouse, as she used to sleep as a child.

Andrew's weight made the mattress dip close to her.

'Do you need me to fetch a doctor?'

'I would not. You never know, I may die and you will be rid of me.' She hated him – *and loved him*.

'Mary?'

She regretted her words. She was not a resentful person like him. 'I am sorry. You need not worry. Thank you for helping me, but it is only a headache. I always seem to have one now. Please leave me to sleep.'

A warm palm pressed on her forehead. It was the most intimate contact they had shared for a long time. 'You feel hot. Let me call for a doctor.'

More tears ran. 'I do not want a doctor. I just need to sleep. Please leave me alone.'

The mattress shook as he got up.

She rolled over so she was lying on his side of the bed, groaning at the throbbing pain.

Then he was there again, his hand on her shoulder. 'I do not think I can leave you like this, sweetheart.'

Oh Lord, it hurts so much. 'Please do not call me sweetheart, leave me alone.' She could not bear to hear kind words from him now she knew they were false. But the nausea rose up. She clutched his wrist. 'I am going to be ill again.'

The chamber pot was placed before her and Mary retched painfully. His palm rested on her shoulder and he whispered soothing words.

Lies, all lies!

'I will not go out this evening. I will stay with you,' he said when she had stopped retching, and he put the chamber pot aside.

She did not argue. It felt as though a farrier were hammering a horseshoe on an anvil in her head.

His fingers pulled at the buttons at the back of her dress.

'Leave me!' she begged.

'Mary, darling, if I release the buttons and loosen your stays, you will be more comfortable. The maid cannot do it as she is not due for hours.'

She lay pitifully still, as he worked the buttons free and pulled the laces loose.

'May I help you take your dress off? You will be more comfortable in your chemise.'

She could smell vomit on her dress too. She sat up and helped him strip off the bodice of her dress and stays, then lifted her bottom so he could slide her dress off over the layers of her petticoats and chemise.

Before she lay down, he untied and removed her petticoats too. Then he helped her climb beneath the sheet and blanket and tucked her in the bed.

Her stomach clenched at the intimacy as misery hollowed out her soul.

The mattress rocked as he sat on his side of the bed, with his back against the headboard and his legs stretched out. His fingers pulled the pins from her hair, then they stroked from her temple to a point behind her ear, gently, over and over.

Her headache began to ease, and sleep slowly claimed her.

16

When Mary's breathing eased to a slow rhythm that implied she had fallen asleep, Drew carefully climbed off the bed. He left the door ajar in case she was sick again.

He went to the chest the decanter stood on and his palms pressed down either side of the silver tray. His head dropped in defeat. That cold, heavy lump of marble in his chest that some people called a heart, kicked.

He had hurt her irrevocably.

She had been stalwart for the last couple of weeks, ignoring his disengagement, and continuing to be kind, even though she spent hardly any time here. But he had started the game of going out. She was simply surviving it – as Caro survived Kilbride's violence.

She is going to leave... Or certainly her aunt had been urging her to go.

I cannot lose her.

Standing straight, his arms lifted, his fingers clasped behind his neck and his head pressed back. He had a feeling her headache was his fault. He thought she would have stayed with her parents as she felt ill. The fact she did not implied she had come here to escape their urging.

This game of tug of war with her family was tearing her apart.

She had told him to leave her alone, and not to call her sweetheart.

Ah God.

All he had done by shutting her out was to convince her he had *never* loved her. Of course, she believed that; he treated her horribly now, behaving like the evil bastard people thought him.

Because that is who I am and she would have seen it in the end – she will go now or later.

But, I cannot let her go.

He sighed, his hands fell and he reached for the decanter.

I will make her want to stay.

* * *

The dinner arrived at six, and Drew sat down and ate alone. The maid arrived at half past the hour of seven. He sent her away, then settled in the chair where he had spent his nights of late, with the bottle of red wine that was sent up with dinner.

He looked at the chessboard, picked up a pawn and rolled it around in his fingers. In recent evenings he had sauntered around gambling dens alone, not gambling because he refused to waste Mary's money. But he had wasted hours until he knew Mary would be in bed. Wasting the time he could have spent with the woman he loved.

What the hell was he running from? The chance of a perfect life.

The deeds to Caro's cottage would be signed over to him in a week and then he planned to move her. He hoped she would be happy there.

And himself? Was he capable of happiness, of making this a good marriage? It was probably too late.

He had convinced himself Mary would find happiness without him. He was unsure of that now. She was deeply unhappy, and he was a heartless bastard, who had brought on her misery.

Neither of us are happy.

He had to try again.

A knock struck the door. He put down the chess piece and glass, and stood. What were the odds it was Marlow, ready to call him out to a duel?

'Peter?' Drew's voice expressed his surprise. It was another man who had good reason to call him out.

Peter's eyebrows lifted. 'Are you going to ask me in, or am I no longer welcome?'

'You may come in, but be quiet, Mary is unwell and sleeping.' Drew stepped back, holding the door open.

Peter's hands pressed into his pockets as he entered.

'Would you like some wine, or brandy?'

Peter sighed. 'Brandy. I need it. I thought you would send me an apology but you are clearly too pig-headed for that. So, I have come to hear it from your lips.'

Drew poured the brandy in silence and handed the glass to Peter, the image of Peter's gloved fingers resting on Mary's back in his head.

Peter's eyebrows lifted. 'It was a waltz,' he said, reading Drew's thoughts. 'Before a hundred or more people. It was no insult. None ought to have been taken.' His free hand rubbed his jaw. 'Remind me to keep you off my face at Jackson's, your right hook is a demon. I prefer you on my side. So, will you apologise or am I still to be cut?'

'I am hardly cutting you, I just poured you a drink.' Drew

dropped into the chair and picked up his wine.

'But you are still angry with me...' Peter sat in the chair Drew now thought of as Mary's. 'As I thought...' he added when Drew did not respond. 'Harry and Mark blame me. They think I broke some law they have invented about touching each other's wives. I personally think if we are to stay friends, when, if, we settle, we ought to make friends of our friends' wives, which is what I intended. Clearly, you think her beneath my friendship.'

'Hardly that.' Drew stared at Peter.

'You could have said you were marrying for love of the woman, as much as money. We would not have judged you for it.'

'Can you imagine, a rake of my reputation falling head over heels for a debutante?'

Peter sighed and leaned forward, resting his elbows on his knees as he sipped from the glass. 'Seriously, you are my friend, I would not take her from you. She was anxious, pacing about this room. I merely escorted her to meet her family.'

'So she said.'

'But you did not believe her?'

'Of course I believed her. It was a bad day. I did not have a clear head. You became caught up in it. I am sorry I hit you.'

'Ah, at last, the apology.' Peter lifted his glass in the form of a toast. 'To being friends... And your wife?'

Drew grimaced. 'Hates me... She is sleeping off a headache in there.' His hand indicated the bedchamber.

'I have seen Mary a lot about town, with her family. And before you think it, I have not spoken to her. Your absence has been noted, though. Society thinks your marriage is on the rocks.'

'It is no one else's business.'

'I am merely saying what I hear. It is not my opinion. Where have you been?'

A bitter sound of amusement broke from Drew's throat. 'Here, there and nowhere, and tonight I am here because my conscience has been kicked. She is leaving me, I think. I overheard her aunt persuading her to go.'

'You will let that happen...? Have you been holding on to this stupid grudge against the both of us for dancing one dance?'

Drew ran a hand through his hair, then dropped it. 'It is not that.'

Peter emptied his glass, stood and walked over to the decanter. He brought it back with him and put that and his glass on the games table. 'Does she know you love her?'

'She does not believe it. I have a certain reputation, you see...'

'And a temper, and a streak of pig-headedness as strong as iron.' Peter leaned down suddenly, pressing a hand on either arm of the chair Drew sat in, looking Drew in the eyes. 'What do you think of Kilbride?'

'What?' Drew looked at Peter with bewilderment.

'Do you approve of his behaviour towards Caro?'

'Of course not. You know I do not.'

'Then what the hell are you doing?'

'What...?' Drew had no idea what Peter meant.

'Have you taken her anywhere since that fracas?'

Drew took a breath, but he was not explaining to Peter how unlovable he felt himself. 'She has her family.'

Peter pushed off the chair and straightened. 'And a husband with a will of iron. You, more than most, should know how painful silence can be. As painful as violence, perhaps. I have watched it change you over the years. You hide its impact, but it hurts.'

Drew would have stood, but Peter pushed him back into the chair. 'I have no desire to fight you, and I am not touching the subject of your family, but you should know that I know how you feel. Do not destroy what you have with this woman. She loves you. It screamed from her the night I came here. She was afraid for you, and making excuses for you, when I presumed you had charged off in a rage.'

Drew did not deny it.

'I hate you, when you're like this,' she had said earlier.

Everything Peter said was endorsed by the words Mary and her aunt had thrown at him earlier.

'I am well aware of the mess I have made of things,' Drew said. 'I was sitting here mulling it over when you arrived.'

Silence was equal to violence. Had he been that dreadful? But it was true.

Drew drank his glass of wine.

Peter reached for the decanter, filled his glass and retook his seat. 'Anyway, I have said my piece, but to be clear, I am not surprised Mary is thinking of deserting you.'

Drew smiled, his lips stiff. 'Yet you have never deserted me.'

'There are times I have thought about it.' He smiled. 'Your stubbornness would test any friendship.'

Drew laughed.

'I saw Caro the other night,' Peter said.

'I am buying her a house,' Drew told him. 'I hope to smuggle her away in secret next week. At least it means some good will have come from my marriage, if Mary's money means Caro is safely settled.'

17

The sound of Drew's laughter woke Mary. He was in the sitting room.

She opened her eyes and sat up. Her limbs felt shaky but the headache was better.

The bedchamber was dark, apart from a line of light from a crack where the door had been left ajar.

'I saw Caro the other night.' Lord Brooke was here. Andrew must have reconciled with his friend.

'I am buying her a house,' Drew told him. 'I hope to smuggle her away in secret next week. At least it means some good will have come from my marriage, if Mary's money means Caro is safely settled.'

It is true! He has a mistress! Mary's empty stomach roiled. She pressed a palm to her mouth and lay back down, afraid of being sick.

She did not cry. The well of her sorrow was dry. She could not continue crying for him forever – nor trying for him.

I will leave.

She could not stay.

Tomorrow, when he rode in the morning, she would leave and this would all be over.

18

Drew held the open door.

'Goodnight. Your wife will come about,' Peter said. 'Do not ignore her, hold your temper and there you have it.'

Drew smiled. 'Goodnight.'

'May Cupid be with you,' Peter said, raising a hand, before walking away.

Drew shut the door, thinking about the day before her father had found them in the inn. That had been a good day, the two of them in harmony. He was still the first few footprints in the snow of her life. He was the only man Mary had known.

He thought of Caro, when they were young, lying in the snow making angel shapes using her arms and legs, making him laugh.

Instead of trying to pull Mary away from her family, he and Mary should have been lying in the crisp fresh snow of their life making angels.

It was the wrong time of year for snow... He laughed at his mental jest. Hay then. They ought to be in fields rolling in the hay.

He would repair this. He would make it right. He would try harder. He would be the person she needed.

He looked at the chair where he had been sleeping. It would do no harm if he shared their bed again. If he slept beside her he would know if she was ill again.

He stripped down to his shirt in the sitting room, so he would not disturb her. Then walked about the room snuffing out the candles. The last one, he picked up and carried into their bedchamber. She was facing the door, on the side of the bed he had always slept, her dark hair tumbling across his pillow, not plaited.

She had taken it over – his bed. His life. His body. His mind. His heart.

He was going to correct every mistake he had made. Every day, he would make sure she knew how he felt. He drew back the sheet, put the candle down on the chest beside the bed and slipped beneath the covers.

He turned and blew out the candle, wrapping them in darkness, then moved closer to her and rested a palm on her hip.

He fell asleep thinking of hay fields, and snow, and how he and Mary would spend their time when they found a property in the country.

19

When Mary woke the grey light said it was barely past dawn. For a moment she thought she was dreaming, but no, Andrew was in bed. He had lain flush against her back, and his palm held her stomach.

She rolled onto her side, looking at him.

He was awake. 'I love you,' he said. Speaking as though he had lain there for a long time looking at her. 'I am sorry I am a fool.'

She had no idea what to say.

'Has your headache gone?'

She nodded.

He kissed her temple, her cheek and the corner of her lips. He stroked the hair from her forehead. 'I will do everything I can to show you I love you. I want to be the man you need. I missed you. I missed spending time with you.'

He leaned forward, his lips pursing. She accepted the kiss as his palm rested on her hip.

'Do you forgive me?' he asked. 'May I make love to you?'

She did not answer.

He kissed her again, this time opening his mouth and using his tongue.

He must have assumed her answer was given by the kiss, because his fingers worked up her nightdress. She did not stop him. The thought of him being in her body again aroused her, desire swelling. It had been so long, and this would be the last time she could know him like this.

A moan of surprise slipped from her throat as his fingers touched between her legs.

She had longed to feel adored for all these days he had not come to her bed.

His teeth nipped at her neck.

He does not love me, she told herself. Yet, her body did not care. This had always worked between them, because when he touched her she believed in his love.

She shut her eyes. She should tell him to stop, but she could not. She wanted to know his lovemaking this one last time.

I love him even if he does not love me. Even if it is a lie, it will be precious to me. It would be one last memory to keep hold of.

His fingers slid into her, only for a moment, before he straightened up and stripped off his shirt. She sat up and removed her chemise.

His own personal musky scent hung in the air as he kissed a path down between her breasts and across her stomach. She shut her eyes tight, she did not want to look at his eyes and see the lies they carried.

He caressed the place between her thighs with his tongue and teeth, and she swirled into the little death, her fingers curling in his soft hair. She preserved every feeling to memory, so she could recall this in the years she would spend alone.

When he slid inside her, the moan that came from her throat was half sob.

He withdrew and pressed back in, coupling with her in an enchanting intimate dance.

'Open your eyes, darling.'

She swallowed back the urge to cry and looked into the shades of amber and honey; not seeing lies there, but love.

He withdrew from her and slid back in, weaving an excruciating bliss into her blood.

'I love you,' he said.

You do not!

'I am such a fool. I will be a better a man, I swear it. We will work things out between us.'

Mary shut her eyes, and let the blissful sensations help her to forget his deceit and betrayal, suspending herself in a moment in time, and expressing her love for him.

As his pace quickened, she clung to his shoulders, her fingertips pressing into his skin at each invasion. It would not be long before she broke again. Her hands ran down his back, feeling the movement of the muscles beneath his skin, reaching to his buttocks. His movement changed from long strokes to a quick pulse. Her thighs clenched as the sound from her mouth became a tremble, and then her conclusion came in a rush.

His muscles locked hard and a deep sound of relief ripped from his throat. Then she could feel him shaking between her thighs. His forehead fell to her shoulder for a moment, and his weight settled more heavily on her.

It was over. She would never know this again.

He withdrew and tumbled onto his back, pulling her on top of him, holding her close.

Her head rested on his chest, in the position she had once thought was heaven.

'I am sorry I hurt you.' His voice rumbled in his chest, as his hand stroked across her hair. 'It will not happen again. It will be different now. I promise. Do not leave me.'

So, that was the reason for this. He was fighting to make her stay. A public separation and divorce would embarrass him. She no longer cared. She planned to go back to her parents' estate and never come back to London.

But for now... she clung to him and pretended to her heart that he loved her as he whispered false promises and talked of finding a home somewhere quiet in the country.

She did not think he noticed she had not spoken.

But when he rolled her onto her back and leaned to kiss her, as though he would make love again, the time had come to stop dreaming and face what was real.

'I am hungry, Andrew.'

He smiled. His caring smile – not the roguish one. 'I am being selfish, keeping you in bed. I have a lot to learn.' He turned away and threw back the covers. 'But I shall learn, Mary. I will get your breakfast. Stay here.'

He got up, gloriously naked, his body so beautiful. He pulled on his shirt, then disappeared. He returned with a plate of buttered bread and sliced ham, and a cup of chocolate.

She sat upright and leaned against the bedhead.

'Would you like to ride with me after breakfast?' he asked, leaving the room again.

'No, thank you!' she called. 'Milly will help me dress while you are gone!' *And help me leave.*

He returned with a full plate for himself and sat at the end of the bed, one knee raised so he faced her, looking as though he had never told a lie in his life.

'Would you rather I stayed here?'

'No.' He had to go out, because she had to leave.

'Then I will go riding and afterwards we will visit your family, thank them for their advice, and tell them we are very happy.'

As soon as the door closed behind him, she dressed herself, ran downstairs and asked Joseph to send someone to hand a letter to the Duke of Pembroke's stables. Then she packed the few things she had removed from her trunks.

Four grooms arrived with the cart she had asked them to bring. It was quickly loaded, with the maid's help too.

Mary placed a note between the chess pieces and looked at Andrew's rooms one last time. Then she closed the door, locked it and slid the key beneath it.

20

Instead of a coin, Drew handed Timmy an iced bun he had bought from a baker. The young street sweep grinned his thanks for the sweet, sticky gift.

The sun seemed brighter today, the sky bluer and the grass greener, because Drew was hopelessly in love with his wife.

Loving her this morning had been divine.

He was a new man, a man who would love her as she deserved.

As she loved him.

She did. Still. Her emotions were in her eyes this morning while they made love. Her heart had been broken by his actions, but she had forgiven him.

He would apologise to her family. He needed them on his side to make this work. Surely, they would stop objecting if they knew he loved her. Perhaps he ought to stand up in the middle of the lion's den and tell them all they were wrong, that he did love Mary and it had never just been because of her money. He tipped his hat to Joseph who was speaking with another resident.

He laughed as he ran upstairs, and swung around the banister onto the landing. The world was a good place with Mary in it. Caro would be proud of him.

He turned the door handle but it was locked. He pulled the key from the pocket of his riding coat, slotted it into the lock and opened the door. 'Mary...' The room was different; her writing desk had gone.

She would not have left... They made love...

He turned to the bedchamber. Everything of hers had gone, apart from the dent hollowed in the pillow where she had slept, and where...

Why did she let me do it?

He walked to the bed, picked up her pillow and held it to his face, smelling the scent of her hair.

She left.

There was nothing he could do. It was over.

He went to the decanter and poured himself a drink to numb the pain that clasped at his heart. The neck of the decanter chimed against the rim of the glass as his hand shook.

Nausea twisted in his gut as he drank the brandy like water.

What had the sex this morning been about? A goodbye gift?

He drank a second glass. Then poured a third and faced the room.

A letter stood balanced among the chess pieces.

His heart dropped like a ton weight. He crossed the room and picked it up.

For her to have cleared out so quickly, her exit must have been arranged with Pembroke's help.

Then why the hell had she let him touch her this morning? He thought this morning was a new beginning, not the end.

He was only worth a couple of sentences of hurried script.

I cannot stay. I have lied to my parents for you since I met you. I cannot carry on living with lies.

Goodbye.

Mary

This morning had been the worst lie of all. She clung to him and came for him... when she could not have wanted him.

Hell! He was an ass. His soul writhed with pain. But a broken heart did not kill a man. It only made him bitter.

He crumpled the paper in his fist and tossed it into the empty hearth. Then dropped into a chair and held his head in his hands.

There would be no happy ending to his life.

It is your own fault. You should have left her alone. You are poisonous! Let her be now, for God's sake. You have done enough harm.

Tears flooded his eyes and spilled onto his cheeks. He was not a man who cried.

He threw himself back in the chair, tipping back his head, trying to release the pain thrashing in his chest.

If this was how she felt these last weeks, no wonder she had gone.

Devil take it! Crying for her, or burying his sorrows in a glass, would change nothing. He sniffed and wiped his cheeks and nose on his handkerchief. He must sell the carriage and the blacks he bought for her and go to the bank.

21

Kate, John's wife, walked across the room and set down a tray on the bedside chest. 'I brought you some lemonade and biscuits. Would you like me to stay with you for a while?'

Mary was sitting on the bed with her knees bent up and her body curled over her legs. She was too agitated to lie down. Her mind could not settle enough to rest. 'Thank you. But I would rather be alone.'

'You have been closeted away all day, why don't you come down to dinner?'

Her mother, a number of her aunts and her cousins, Eleanor and Margaret, had come to the room to speak to her; offering comfort and setting aside the marriage they had all predicted would fail. It was, apparently, an unfortunate situation that should be filed quietly away as history.

When she arrived with all her possessions, Aunt Jane told her parents Andrew had been seen with a woman. Her father held her and told her he would publish a notice in the newspaper announcing the separation, to manage any gossip and ensure she was no longer tied to Andrew's reputation.

She did not care. She had no intention of stepping out in public again. When she told him that, he did not believe her. 'You will in time. Time will heal.'

He was wrong. Andrew's scent lingered on her skin from their lovemaking this morning. Time would take that away and her memories would fade, but her love would never ebb.

Her forehead dropped onto her knees and silent tears spilled from her eyes. All she had done since she reached here was cry.

Her mother sat beside her for the first hour, until Mary asked to be left alone. But her family were unable to stay away, every half hour someone would come up to see how she fared, each of them bringing fresh words of reassurance.

None of their words could give her the Andrew she loved. The words he whispered as she had lain on his chest held more weight in her heart than any her family said. She wanted the man who cared for her last night and made love to her this morning – not the man who had betrayed her.

Why did he make love to me?

This morning, he had promised to be different, to make a home with her.

As well as buying a home for his other woman.

Kate's fingers touched Mary's shoulder. 'Drink a little lemonade and eat. We can all see you have lost weight these last weeks.'

Like an automated toy, Mary lifted her head, reached for the glass and sipped; hoping that obeying would make Kate go away.

Kate sat on the edge of the mattress, looking at Mary. 'What will you do?'

'I asked Papa to take me home, but he said he cannot today or tomorrow as he has business in town.'

'Are you sure what Jane said is correct?'

Mary smiled weakly. Trust Kate not to jump to conclusions,

her sister-in-law had a tender heart. She gave people a chance. She had saved John from himself, with her refusal to accept him at face value. She was the first one not to begin by saying that leaving Andrew was the right decision.

'It is true. I heard him talking of his mistress to his friend last night. He is buying a house for her with my dowry.'

'Oh dear...' Kate took the glass from Mary's hand, then held her hand. 'I was convinced of his good intent of late. He may have stepped back from speaking to us but he was being kind to you.'

'We made love this morning.' The words spilled out. 'As though there were nothing wrong. He has not touched me since he hit Lord Brooke. He has slept in a chair in the other room. Then this morning...' She sighed and wiped a tear off her cheek. 'But yesterday he heard Aunt Jane telling me to leave, so I suppose he wants to avoid the embarrassment of a divorce... And he is not here, begging me to come back, is he? Probably because he can go to his mistress now.'

'Have you told your mother this?' Affection weighted Kate's voice and softened her gaze.

'No, and do not. Papa or John would attack him. It is bad enough as it is.'

Kate nodded. 'Anything you say to me will stay between us.'

'He is so believable,' Mary said. 'The look in his eyes expresses love, and when he touches me, it feels real; it feels as though he treasures me. I thought he loved me when I ran away with him. He said he did. He spoke in the way he did this morning. He is bitter inside, Kate, and stubborn, and short-tempered, but he is also kind. He even said Papa and John have a right to hate him, he did not hold their anger against them. Though, I know Andrew was spiteful at times.

'Did you see how he was when he came here that afternoon? He looked lost. That day I asked to meet his family and even though he did not wish to, he took me there. They are horrible. They threw us out. That was the day he hit Lord Brooke. He stopped pretending to love me after that. But then this morning he changed again.

'I thought I understood him; now I know I just believed his lies. Yet I still love him. Do you think there was always someone else? Do you think he loves this other woman, and only wanted my money?'

Kate's fingers held Mary's tighter, offering comfort. 'How can we know?'

'I will always love him, and...' She had told no one this. 'I think I am carrying his child. Please do not tell Mama and Papa, not yet, I need time to navigate this.'

'Oh, Mary. I will not tell.' Kate released Mary's hand and hugged her instead. 'All will be well. You have us all to help you.'

Mary had no idea what Andrew would do when he found out about their child. This was her pain, her secret – that she carried a child created with a man who did not love her. She could not hide the pregnancy forever, but she could hide herself; that is what she wished to do, hide away and pretend this had not happened. At least for now.

She pulled away from Kate and wiped the tears from her cheeks.

'John and I told lies too,' Kate admitted. 'After the party he held in Ashford, while you were at the end of your mourning for your grandfather, we made love. I went to him because I loved him. He did not love me then, but I fell pregnant and John did the honourable thing. He loves me now, Mary.'

'Of course he loves you.' Mary clutched Kate's hand. 'I see it in his eyes every time he looks at you.'

Kate smiled. 'I know. I did not tell you because I need your reassurance. I said it so you would know things are not always what they seem. Perhaps things will work out for you too.'

'He has a mistress, Kate.'

'And you are carrying a child which you both made. At some point you must tell him. The child must know its father. I once intended to marry another man and keep my child a secret from John, and you have seen how he adores Paul, it would have been cruel of me.'

Mary sighed. Kate's mother had taken her own life; Kate knew what it was like when a child did not know its parent.

'Why not come home to Pembroke Place with John and I? You may have time alone to think things over and heal a little, without the noise of all the children. We can go tomorrow. John can still travel into the city to attend the House of Lords. Then, when you feel able, I can help you talk to Andrew about the child.'

'I would prefer not to see anyone else. I know it is selfish.'

'It is not selfish. People will understand.'

Mary wiped her cheeks again and smiled. 'Thank you.'

'Now eat those biscuits, you must think of the child as well as yourself. I will tell John our plans.'

'Will he mind?'

'You know he will not. He would do anything for you, he loves you dearly, and he prefers being on the estate anyway, he will be glad of an excuse to go.'

'Thank you.'

'You need not thank me. You are my sister. Our home is your home.'

'Would you send Mama to me, so I can tell her I will stay with you.'

22

It had taken two weeks to get the deeds signed over and organise a date, time and place to help Caro escape. Now the day had come, his stomach was in turmoil.

Drew met her in Mayfair, at the gate of the backyard of Madame Duval's modiste's, to make it look to Kilbride's staff as though she were simply shopping. She hurried through the back gate. 'Caro.' He kissed her cheek and took her shaking hand. 'Come.' He led her along the alley. 'Did the modiste query your exit?'

'No. I asked if I might use her closet. But there is a footman waiting in the shop.'

'Then we must hurry.' Drew opened the gate and they ran along the narrow back alley. 'I ordered the carriage under a false name. We will change the carriage once we are out of London and go the opposite way. Then change again, so we cannot be easily followed. Where was Kilbride when you left?'

'In the House of Lords. They will be sitting for hours and none of the servants will be able to speak to him there.'

The carriage door stood ajar so they could ascend quickly. He handed her in and climbed in behind her. 'Go!' he yelled up to the driver as he shut the door. The carriage jolted forward and he fell into the seat beside Caro.

'Pull down the blind,' he told her, drawing down the one beside him.

Caro's hands trembled and she breathed heavily from the effort of their flight. She withdrew a folded silk handkerchief from her reticule and looked at him. 'I brought something to help.' She unfolded the silk parcel that lay in her lap. Gold and jewels glinted in the low light of the carriage. 'They are all gifts he gave me, they are mine to take, earbobs, hair slides, bracelets and necklaces.'

Drew smiled awkwardly, he had not expected her to bring anything. 'I will sell them for you, they will help you live for years.'

He had not told her his circumstances had changed. He thought if he did, she would refuse to leave. So, the money from her trinkets would be handy.

Drew leaned to the window and lifted the edge of the blind with a fingertip. They were passing the shopfront and Kilbride's carriage. There were no panicked servants surrounding it; the footman must still be waiting patiently inside.

The journey out of London was fast and easy; all went according to plan. When they arrived in Maidstone, the house-keeper was there, waiting to settle Caro in.

The cottage was small. There were two rooms downstairs, a kitchen and a parlour, and two upstairs, with an attic for the housekeeper. He had arranged for the housekeeper to purchase everything she and Caro would need, from clothing and furniture to food and candles.

Knowing Caro was afraid of what was to come, he stayed with

her for a couple of hours and drank tea with her in the sitting room.

While Caro got to know the housekeeper, his thoughts drifted to the fond memories he nurtured of Mary. He had not thought of her for most of the day... but now... he remembered all the commonplace moments they spent like this. He missed her. He longed for peaceful moments with her. Even to sit in her brother's drawing room and drink tea with her. But hope had passed.

'Drew...'

He smiled at Caro. 'Sorry, I was wool gathering...' The truth was he had barely slept since Mary left and his mind was a mess, but he lay no blame on her. All the blame was his.

Caro held his hand for a moment.

It was laughable... the two of them. He had once thought Mary was life's flotsam. No. She was protected and loved by the numerous members of her family. He and Caro were the flotsam – two drifting souls.

'I should leave.' Drew stood. 'I must return to London, so Kilbride will not guess I helped you. It may be weeks before I can return; Kilbride will have people watching me. So, do not write, it is not worth the risk. I will come as soon as I can, and in the meantime, do not draw attention to yourself.'

She nodded. Then she stood and hugged him. 'Thank you.'

'You must be brave, stay calm and strong. He will not find you, I promise.'

'I am very grateful.'

'I am glad I have finally been able to help you.'

23

Several hours later, Drew climbed the steps of Sheffield's town house with Peter by his side. They were attending Sheffield's ball because he knew Kilbride would be looking for him, and he was sending a silent, very public, message – *you will not find her*.

But there was another reason he was here – he hoped for a glimpse of Mary.

He and Peter had attended several balls since she left, so he might see her, to know she was well, and quieten the screams of his soul. He had not encountered her once. The last time he laid eyes on her was the day she left – the day they had lain together as though they were in love.

That morning still haunted him. He did not understand why she let that happen.

Emotions tore at him as they entered the ballroom. He wanted to plead with her, to persuade her to come back. But if he saw her, he had promised himself he would not speak. She was better off without him.

Peter looked over his shoulder. 'I do not think she is here.'

'I doubted it anyway; but it does not stop me wishing.'

Peter's palm rested on Drew's shoulder. 'I told you to write to her. I am sure Marlow would pass it on.'

'More likely he would burn it, and if he did not Mary would.'

Peter's hand fell away. 'You were an ass, my friend. But I still do not understand why you gave the money back.'

'It seemed wrong to keep it. It was her money.'

'Not legally.'

'Who cares about legality? I wish I could give it all back, but I had paid my debts and I need money to support Caro.'

'Still, I bet it shocked them.'

'I doubt it. I think my name is a swear word in Pembroke's house. Regardless, I need to do something with my life. If she wants a divorce I will let her have it, but I will not marry again. I am done with women, and very grateful for the offer of employment. I shall happily bury myself in the country with your horses.'

'You have an eye for horses and a skill for training them. I am doing myself a favour not you. With you managing the stud, I will have the best racers out there,' Peter finished as they crossed the threshold into the brilliant light of the ballroom.

He stopped still and looked around the room. Neither Mary nor her parents were there, but her aunts and uncles, the Wiltshires, Bradfords and Barringtons, were in attendance. He had seen them all before, but not Pembroke or Marlow.

The Duke of Arundel glared at Drew.

Drew's guts twisted. What had Mary told them?

They had hated him before; they must despise him now.

Wiltshire turned his back, in a cutting gesture. The gesture was nothing to a man whose own mother refused to acknowledge his existence.

Speaking of that, she was here too, with the Marquis and Drew's eldest brother and his wife. They had probably notched his separation up as one of their achievements; by making Mary see how pathetic he was.

'Kilbride is here,' Peter said. 'And so is my sister. Come along, she will tell us about any rumours.'

Even though Wiltshire had turned away, Drew sensed the man's gaze following him. He was getting used to the sensation of invisible daggers striking his back.

'Hayley,' Peter called.

She walked across to them, as they were a little distant from the crowd.

Peter kissed her cheek. 'What is going on tonight? Is there anything we should know?'

She held out her hand to Drew, he bowed over it. He had known her since their childhood, when he spent his first summer away from the boarding school with Peter's family.

She smiled as he straightened. 'You are the gossip, Drew; since that announcement. I believe your wife has left town. Certainly, both the Duke of Pembroke and Lord Marlow have gone. You men, you do like to make us women suffer.'

'She left me.' Belligerence burned in Drew's voice. He had not expected them to announce the separation. 'I thought their announcement made that clear.' He schooled his voice, he did not want the world to know how hurt he was.

Hayley's fan tapped his upper arm. 'And you are entirely innocent, I suppose. She left you for no reason at all.'

'None that I can think of.' His tone turned dry.

Hayley's gaze passed over his shoulder and her eyes widened. Her fingers clutched his sleeve. 'Have you some grievance with the Marquis of Kilbride? He is coming this way with a thunderous look on his face.'

'The jig is up,' Peter said.

'Lord Framlington!' The Marquis of Kilbride's bellow rang

out, his voice booming over the orchestra's music. The conversations near them ceased.

Drew knew this scene would come, but he thought Kilbride would challenge him in private; he had not expected him to do so at a ball. It never occurred to him it would happen in front of Mary's kin. This would add fuel to her family's fire.

Setting a twisted be-damned smile on his lips, Drew faced his fate. Perhaps having this out in public was preferential. In private Kilbride would have brought his thugs and dumped Drew's broken body in a back alley. He had made a will in case that should happen and left the cottage to Caro, so even if Kilbride killed him, he would not win.

Of course, Mary's money had bought the cottage, so it should go to her, but he could not leave Caro unprotected.

Drew stiffened his spine, stretching up the two inches he had over his brother-in-law. 'Is there something you want to say to me?' he asked Kilbride.

'You know there is!' Kilbride bellowed at full pitch, speaking as though he were in the House of Lords.

'Forgive me, but, no. You have me at a disadvantage...' Drew let a smirk play on his lips, taking pleasure in watching Kilbride's anger. Let him hit a man for a change, it would give Drew the chance to hit him back.

'You have stolen my wife! You incestuous bastard!' Kilbride's words echoed around the room and now even the music had stopped.

Drew's vision tainted red and his hands curled to fists. *Lord!* That was the last thing he had expected to be accused of.

'It is no wonder your wife deserted you! She knew you for a wretch! She caught you in bed with my wife! Your sister!'

Drew's control cracked. He lunged at Kilbride, grabbing his lapel with his left hand and striking with his right fist. He hit bone, probably breaking his brother-in-law's nose. The noise about him was a vague sound as his fist struck Kilbride's jaw. Kilbride threw a pathetic punch in return, which Drew dodged.

Someone pulled at his arm, and a voice growled near his ear, 'If you kill him, you will hang.' Peter.

The red mist faded as Peter's words pulled Drew back to his senses.

He thrust Kilbride away so hard, the man fell to the floor and scrabbled around like a fish out of water. 'I will see you swing for this and I will find her!' Kilbride spat.

Drew dropped to his haunches and held Kilbride's arm as though he was going to help him up. Instead, he held him down. 'Do whatever you want, you will not find her.'

Drew stood then, and yanked Kilbride to his feet. A hundred faces swam about him as Drew let go of Kilbride's arm. As he turned away women rushed forward to console Kilbride, while the men glared at Drew, and at the front of them, Wiltshire, and beside him Barrington and Bradford.

'Incestuous!' Drew heard the outraged word on someone's lips. One woman spat at him.

His gaze caught on his mother's. She stood towards the back of the crowd. His brother stood beside her, looking down his nose as though he smelt horse dung.

'Incestuous...' The word was repeated.

A wave of sound rippled through the crowd as the gossip spread.

'For God's sake, get out of here,' Peter whispered, his hand pressing on Drew's back.

Before Drew could move, someone grasped his left arm. 'You have brought shame on my niece.' Wiltshire. 'If this is true, if you have tangled Mary up in this... God help me... I will kill you myself.'

Drew pulled his arm loose.

'Let us have music!' Barrington shouted from beyond Wiltshire, gesturing to the orchestra. Bradford was speaking with Kilbride. No doubt Kilbride was pouring poison into his ear.

'Go back to your dancing!' Barrington shouted at the observers who hovered.

Drew had been found guilty in Wiltshire's eyes. Mary would know of this by the morning. But she hated Drew anyway. He shrugged off his anger. 'Go to hell, Wiltshire,' he hissed through his teeth then walked away.

Peter followed. 'Expect to be called out by a dozen men in the morning. I would not go anywhere near White's for a month or two.'

People looked at Drew as though he really was the devil, before turning their backs.

'That will do no good,' Drew answered as they reached the hall. 'They know where I live.'

'Then leave London.' Peter was deadly serious. 'Go to my country estate now.'

A footman opened the door and they stepped out into the night, before a lynch mob had the chance to form. But Peter was right, Drew's comeuppance would come tomorrow.

'They can do what they like.'

'So now you have a death wish.'

Drew did not answer as they descended the steps. He looked for Peter's carriage among the line of those waiting. If Mary's family wanted to have their revenge and challenge him to a duel, he would not fight; he would delope, and fire his shot into the air. If they shot him they would be doing him a favour. He could not imagine living the rest of his life bearing this much inner pain. He had freed Caro. What happened to him did not matter.

Peter's hand settled on Drew's shoulder. 'I am not ready to

part with you, my friend. Do not do anything foolish, and tonight I would suggest you get very drunk, and as your best friend I am willing to help you achieve that. Let us find Mark and Harry, they will willingly help you too, and then you are sleeping at my house. No one is going to shoot you. And believe me, I shall be telling everyone tomorrow you are not an incestuous man.'

'As though they will believe you...' Drew laughed, but it was a broken sound.

24

John reeled back, shocked. 'Good God. That bastard!'

Mary looked at John. He was reading a letter at the breakfast table. It was unlike John to express his emotions so vehemently.

'John!' Kate whispered.

Mary put her cup of chocolate down. John was looking at her. Whatever had made him angry was something to do with her.

His expression changed to a look of regret. 'I am sorry.'

'Why?' she asked.

So far, the child had been kind to her; she had only suffered slight nausea in the mornings and never been physically ill, but now she felt as if she might be sick.

John's gaze ran around the footmen about the table. 'Leave us, please.' They bowed deeply then filed out. 'You too, Finch,' John prompted the butler.

Mary had never seen him send the servants from the room.

A hand pressed to her stomach, as though she would protect the child from whatever was coming. John stood.

She stood too, with a desire to run. 'Please, do not tell me. I do not wish to know if he has been seen with her.'

'Mary.' John came closer. 'You must know this. The letter is from Uncle Richard, and you must hear this from me and not others. It is worse than you thought. Sit down.'

She did, her legs too weak to hold her.

John's gaze softened as he sat in the dining chair beside her. 'Uncle Richard saw Lord Framlington at a ball last night. He was involved in another brawl and an accusation was thrown, which everyone heard.'

'Is the woman married?'

'She is.' He looked sorrowful. 'It is the Duchess of Kilbride, his sister Caroline. He was accused of incest by his brother-in-law, and his sister has disappeared. It is said they have been in a physical relationship for years.'

'Good Lord.' Kate's fingers covered her mouth.

It is not true. Mary shook her head. 'John, it is not true. He would not.'

'You told me his family have cut him,' Kate said. 'They also cut the Duchess of Kilbride. This would explain why, if their family knew...'

Mary looked at Kate. 'That is absurd. It is not true! He would not do such a thing. I saw him speaking with the Duchess of Kilbride once, before we wed. They had been talking outside—'

'Is that not added proof?' John said in a kind voice, as though he thought she simply did not want to believe it.

'No.' Her voice grew stronger. 'Andrew told me Lord Kilbride beat her, and all he could do was offer comfort. He was the only person she trusted. I saw bruises on her neck once after that and they looked like finger marks. Lord Kilbride will have said that because Andrew has helped his sister.'

Mary shut her eyes and felt the blood drain from her skin. Suddenly everything made sense. She opened her eyes and looked at Kate. 'The woman in the draper's... That was her! She wears veils to hide the bruises.'

Mary stood. 'He bought the house for her! He said, Caro. Caroline. His sister. I did not make the connection. He does not have a mistress, Kate! Oh, Kate, he made love to me and said he was sorry, that he would try to prove himself, and I left him.'

Mary looked at John. 'You must take me back. I must go to him.'

John's expression became uncertain. 'You cannot. He has gone into hiding. Kilbride wants him hanged. Although as far as I know there is no charge against him yet.'

She shook her head. 'He will not hide from them, that is not Andrew. He will not run. If they accuse him, he will look them in the eye and tell them all to go to hell, not hide.'

John's lips twitched at one corner. 'That is what he said to Uncle Richard.'

'Then Mary is right, John, if she knows him so well.' Kate pressed. 'And if Mary cannot go to him, we ought to bring him here. If he loves Mary he will come and they can hide from these rumours and resolve the rift between them while the gossip dies down.'

Kate's gaze caught Mary's. 'There is something else you ought to know, which I believe now indicates Lord Framlington's innocence. John and I discussed it and we thought it better not to tell you. But now... Your father and mother know this too and agreed we should not tell you. But Mary, when you came back, it was the same day John and your father received cheques from Lord Framlington. He returned most of your dowry, with a letter that stated he could not keep it if he did not have you. He said it would only be a bitter reminder of what he had lost. John thought it a ploy to win you back, and yet we were not sure because he asked John not to tell you. At the time it made your father and John doubt their judgement. Yet knowing he had a mistress, we thought it would confuse things for you.'

'Were we wrong, Mary?' John touched her shoulder.

'Yes.' He understood at last. 'Andrew never argued against the things you said, John. I think he thought it lowering to defend himself. Yet he told me he loved me a dozen times, and I did not always believe him because you told me he was lying to win my dowry. If it was not for my dowry, then it is true.'

'What you felt was real, Mary. Andrew loved you.' Kate looked at John. 'Mary cannot go to London, so we must bring him here.'

'I will have a carriage prepared.'

'I will come with you,' Kate said. 'He may not be willing to speak with you, John.'

25

Peter threw a newspaper on to Drew's lap. 'Pembroke is back in town, and apparently he is turning over every stone in search of you.'

Drew had sat in Peter's town house in Mayfair for two days, figuratively kicking his heels.

This morning, Peter went out early, scouting for news of how things stood, while Drew sat there twiddling his thumbs. He had tried playing solitaire with a pack of cards but his mind kept wondering what Mary thought of this latest rumour.

Incest.

It was immoral and illegal.

If she believed it... He pushed away the thought as too unbearable. She was the only one whose good opinion he cared for.

'Pembroke is on the war path. He is visiting everywhere, demanding to know if you are there, or if anyone knows where you are.' Peter walked over to his decanters. 'While Kilbride has a rough-looking sort of man standing outside your rooms waiting for you to return. And Wiltshire... well, he has put a sum on your head to have you found. Kilbride, I believe, just wants you dead.'

'He can kill me. Caro is safe, he will not find her.' Drew had not taken a single risk. Even Peter did not know where Caro was.

'I know you do not care.' Peter held up a decanter by its neck, asking if Drew wanted a glass. 'But I do, and I am not going to let anyone kill you.'

Drew nodded, accepting the offer of the drink.

Peter turned to pour. 'I made it public in White's that I, who happen to know you very well indeed, believe the whole story is a pile of horse dung. My brother-in-law is speaking for you in Brooke's Gentlemen's Club and Harry has raised it in Watier's. Our version will be circulated too.'

'Your version?'

A glass in each hand, Peter walked over. 'We are spreading the truth, that Kilbride was beating Caro. It will grow like a snowball. People will have guessed it previously but will have been too cowed by Kilbride to say. Wait and see. The truth will out now.'

'But a man may beat his wife, that is legal.' Drew accepted a glass. 'How long do you think it will take someone to guess I am here?'

'I will go out again this evening, and Mark and Harry can stay with you. That will throw people off the scent, and to help, I am asking people if they have seen you too.'

This was a hell of a muddle.

'My lords.'

Drew and Peter looked at the butler who had opened the door.

'There is a woman downstairs, Lord Brooke, who is asking to speak to you. She came to the servants' door with a letter for you, but she will not pass it on to anyone but yourself, sir.'

Beyond Brooke's butler they heard quick steps. The woman,

who was swamped by a voluminous cloak, was no longer down-stairs but rushing past the butler into the room. She threw the hood back.

Pembroke's wife.

Her hand lifted from beneath the folds of the cloak.

Drew set down his glass and stood, facing the possibility that she had hidden a pistol beneath the cloak.

Peter moved too, preparing to make her drop whatever weapon she held.

But the thing her hand revealed was paper.

A letter.

'I am not here to cause harm, Lord Framlington. Mary told us the truth of this ridiculous tale. John and I have been searching for you, to ask you to travel back with us. Mary is living with us, she wants you there. You will be safer away from London. She would have come to London herself but John and I thought it better that she stayed away. I promised to bring you back. Will you come with us?'

Drew stared at her. The Duchess of Pembroke had come through the servants' entrance to offer him help. She had no reason to help him.

'This letter is from Mary.' She held it out for him to take.

He accepted the letter, his heart hammering.

My dearest Andrew,

I am sorry I did not believe you. I believe you now. Come, come quickly. John will take you out of London and bring you here, where you will be safe.

Mary, your devoted wife.

Will you forgive me for my lack of faith?

He looked up at the Duchess. 'Where is she?'

'At Pembroke Place, not far from London, it is John's principal estate. The house and grounds are extensive. No one will be able to attack you there. You will have time and privacy to resolve these matters with Mary.'

'Is Lord Marlow there also?'

'No, Lord and Lady Marlow have gone to their own estate.'

Your devoted wife.

Does she love me still?

He covered his mouth with his hand and rubbed his chin.

'Mary will be distraught if you do not come. I promised.' Determination glinted in her eyes.

'Where is the Duke? Why are you here and not him?'

'He is waiting a hundred yards away, in an unmarked carriage. John has asked for you everywhere. I said no one is telling him the truth because they think he means harm. I told him I had more chance of persuading Lord Brooke to speak.'

'If I go out there, will I receive a bullet in my chest?'

The Duchess glanced at the letter in his hand. 'Would Mary lie to you? I told you the truth; John and I want you to come for Mary's sake. Mary left you because she overheard a conversation between you and Lord Brooke about a property you purchased for another woman. John's aunt believed you were with a mistress in a draper's warehouse.

'Mary now understands that was your sister. If you are guilty of anything, it is of not telling Mary what you have been doing. She did not leave you for lack of love. She has been inconsolable.'

Drew looked at Peter.

'Go,' Peter said. 'This is what you want; to have her back. My horses will have to manage without you.'

Drew looked at the Duchess. 'I will fetch my bag.'

An hour later, his bag stored in the box, Drew was in a carriage barrelling along the main road from London to Canterbury. Pembroke was seated beside him, with the Duchess seated opposite. It was the same road he had travelled with Caro.

With his arms folded over his chest and the brim of his hat tipped low to hide his eyes, Drew lounged in his seat, the sole of one boot resting on the far seat, the other on the floor, to prevent himself from rocking and sliding with each bump in the road.

Apart from acknowledging Drew as he had handed the Duchess up into the carriage, Pembroke had not said a word. But his eyes had studied Drew as though he were an absurdity. Drew had resisted the urge to stare back, and tilted the rim of his hat down.

Mary used to look at him like that sometimes, when she was trying to understand him. He did not like Pembroke doing it.

Hope breathed, as they travelled, that silent quiet beast of an emotion.

Does she love me?

His whole body was tense with the longing to see her.

The Duchess had attempted to open conversations on bland subjects such as, 'I hope you are comfortable? This carriage is usually used by the servants.' 'At least the weather has held. I hope it will only take a couple of hours to reach Pembroke Place' and 'The parkland there is beautiful.' Eventually her well of obsequious conversation ran dry.

Pembroke coughed. It was an odd sound, half cough, half chuckle. 'Mary knows you fairly well, does she not, Framlington?'

Drew's fingers tilted the brim of his hat up. 'In what way, Your Grace?'

'When I told her our uncle's account of the incident with Kilbride, she said you would not run but tell them to go to hell. I had not told her yet that you said those words to our uncle. Are you sitting here wishing me to hell too?'

Drew held Pembroke's penetrating blue gaze. 'I am doing my best not to, Your Grace, as you are helping me.'

Pembroke's lips lifted in a brief smile. 'Have I judged you wrong, Lord Framlington?'

'You will have to decide that.' Drew tipped his hat back down and looked out the window.

'Mary also said you will not defend yourself.'

Mary ought to keep her mouth shut. Drew did not answer, or look back, but a humorous sound broke from Pembroke's throat.

Drew shut his eyes and pretended to sleep.

26

Pembroke tapped Drew's arm. 'We are here, Framlington.'

Drew must have fallen asleep.

He straightened up, both feet settling on the floor, his heart thumping as hope breathed heavily inside him.

The carriage raced along a broad avenue, and as the avenue swung to the right Drew caught his first glimpse of Pembroke Place. The Palladian property sat like a beast on a ridge in the landscape, dominating the land about it.

He knew Pembroke was wealthy but he had not imagined this. Drew had housed Mary in a two-room apartment in St James. He would lay odds on the fact her bedchamber here was the size of his whole apartment.

The horses' hooves and the carriage wheels crunched in the gravel as the carriage stopped in front of the ostentatious mansion. A broad portico, with long shallow steps and tall stone columns, fronted the property. A set of doors suitable for giants opened inwards.

Drew's stomach dropped and his heartbeat became erratic.

A dozen men in Pembroke's livery hurried towards the carriage. They must have seen the carriage coming from a distance.

A flutter of pink muslin caught his eye. Mary had run from the house.

'Mary.' He opened the door before a footman could and jumped down without the step.

She raced down the shallow steps, decorum forgotten.

He raced to her too, met her midway and as she flung her arms about his neck with a fierce cry of joy, he hugged her middle and lifted her off the ground. He hugged her hard, with relief. He thought he would never hold her again. His cheek pressed against her hair as the embrace of her arms wrapped about his soul too, and her head rested on his shoulder.

'I am sorry,' she said.

She had lost weight, he could feel her spine and her ribs beneath her gown.

His fingers splayed in her hair. 'You have nothing to be sorry for. I am sorry. I could not bear for you to see the real me. I thought you must hate me. That you could never love me. I pushed you away to avoid the pain of you choosing to leave me. I regret it.' He pressed a kiss on the crown of her hair.

She stepped back, her arms lowering. There were tears on her cheeks.

He smiled as tears clouded his vision too.

'You are not hurt,' she said. She ran her hands across his chest, as though she could see through his waistcoat, looking for wounds.

'No.' His fingers lifted her chin, raising her gaze to his face. 'Mary, I am fine. No holes.' He wiped the tears from her cheeks with his thumbs. Then smiled as her fingers wiped his cheeks dry. 'I have been an ass. Caro told me so too.'

He held Mary again, absorbing the scent of her, and pressed another kiss on her hair. Then he met Pembroke's gaze.

Pembroke stood a few feet away, watching with that hint of a smile.

Drew took a deep breath. It would not be easy to let her family see who he really was. It would make him vulnerable. Yet, he had to. Mary's family were important to her and she was important to him, he had to trust in that.

They were devoted to Mary, and so was he. If she loved and trusted these people with her life and happiness, it would be crass of him not to trust them too.

He left one arm about her shoulders and nodded at Pembroke as they walked towards the house, ignoring the discomfort flooding his veins.

The Duchess slipped an arm about Pembroke's midriff, and they walked together too.

'Shall we stay outside for a while and talk?' Mary said.

'If that is what you want to do, sweetheart.'

'Dinner will be served at six. You do not need to dress. It is just the four of us,' the Duchess advised.

Mary lifted Drew's hat off his head and held it out. 'Please take this and Lord Framlington's gloves inside,' she said to a servant.

Smiling, Drew pulled off his gloves and handed them over.

'Let us walk to the lake.' She caught his hand and pulled him onwards, leaving the Pembrokes and their multitude of servants behind.

'Is this where you grew up?' he asked.

'No, my father has an estate, but it is nothing like this. Papa's property is a small manor house with farmland. We used to come here once or twice a year to stay when grandfather was alive, but never for long because Papa and Mama didn't like him very much. But since John has owned Pembroke Place, we come often. I love the grounds. In the summer when all the family are here it is fun.

'How is your sister?' she asked.

He had doubted her belief in him from the moment Marlow had found them at the inn; thought her incapable of loving the damaged man he was. Yet when rumour had him at his lowest – incestuous – without any moral fibre at all, Mary believed him innocent.

Drew glanced back, looking at the house. Pembroke and his staff had gone.

He stopped walking, tugging their joined hands and smiling as he pulled her closer. Then he kissed her. A long deep kiss, weighted with feeling, love gripping at his heart.

When he ended it, a wide smile parted her lips.

He walked on, her hand in his. 'Caro is shaken and afraid. It took an enormous amount of courage for her to leave. It will take her considerable time, I think, to feel safe and settled. She is scared Kilbride will find her. If he ever did, I would be frightened for her. He beat her on the last occasion, because she miscarried his child.'

'Where is she?'

'If I tell you, it puts you in danger. Kilbride's cronies might hurt you for the information.'

'You think I would tell...' She looked hurt.

'No, Mary. But I do not want to endanger you any more than I would risk him finding Caro. But if you must know, she is not far from here.'

'I would like to meet her.'

'Not any time soon, sweetheart. I am not going near her for a long while, just to be safe. Kilbride is like your brother, he has money and men everywhere.'

For a moment the only sounds were the swishes of the long blades of grass giving way beneath their feet as they walked on.

The hill flowed down to an ornamental lake in the distance.

'I am sorry,' Mary said. 'I overheard you talking to Lord Brooke. I thought you had a mistress. You were not coming to bed and...'

Drew did not care to think of the agony she must have felt. 'I responded ridiculously to your dance with Peter, and there you were thinking I had done far worse.' He squeezed her hand. 'The Duchess told me what you heard and what your aunt said. I do not blame you for thinking it, I should have told you.'

'You were not talking to me then.'

'No, as I said. I was an ass.'

'You are friends with Peter again...'

'He came that night, he knows my tendency to sulk and stew, he gave me time to get over it. Your sister-in-law found me at Peter's.'

His fingers wove between hers as they walked on.

The heads of clover they disturbed among the grass sent sweet perfume into the air.

When they reached the lake, they walked along the shore a little way.

The water was as still as glass, a mirror reflecting the summer sky, until a pair of swans with trailing signets glided across it, sending out fans of ripples on the surface.

'I feel like I have walked from a nightmare into a dream.' He looked at Mary. 'Did I fall asleep at Peter's?'

She lifted their joined hands and pressed a kiss on the back of his. 'I am real.'

Drew remembered their last morning with painful guilt. 'Why did you let me make love to you that morning? I thought...' A lump constricted his throat at the memory. He coughed and began again. 'I thought you forgave me. Then... I did not like myself when I found you gone. I dreaded that... Did you feel forced?' His fingers touched her cheek. 'You broke my heart.'

'My heart broke too.' Her fingers slipped from his and she walked ahead of him. 'I love you; just one last time I wanted to pretend you loved me too.'

'You stupid girl.' He rushed her, to break the melancholy, grasping her from behind, trapping her in his arms and lifting her off her feet. 'If I am an ass, you are a fool. I was not pretending. I adore you, woman. You may get that into your silly head, if you please.'

She was laughing breathlessly when he set her down.

'Let us sit for a while,' he suggested.

While he unbuttoned his morning coat and shrugged it off, she picked a single buttercup and spun the stem between her fingers. He lay his coat on the ground for her to sit on, ignoring the fact he had no valet to repair any damage.

She swept her dress beneath her and sat among the long grass. If he was a painter, he would paint her portrait just like this.

Drew lay down, stretching out beside her, on his side, his head supported on his palm. The nonchalant pose denied the raging melee of emotions in his chest.

'Why did you act so differently towards me after we visited your parents?' she asked, as she looked at the lake.

His view was her profile, against the blue sky. 'My parents are an untouchable subject. Peter will tell you not to converse on it.'

She looked at him. 'Andrew...?'

'Mary.' He broke off a stem of long grass and brushed the tip across her nose. She made a face which said, *tell me*.

'So, you insist I go there even though I said I hate the subject.'

Her arms wrapped about her knees, her vulnerability showing through, the buttercup bobbing in her hand. 'Are we going to argue, when we have only just been reunited? If you tell me, I will not need to ask again.'

'If you meet Caro, she will tell you about our parents.' Emotionally naked, he took her left hand from its grip about her knees and held it up between them. His thumb pushed up the third finger that bore his ring, with the little leather cord wrapped about it to hold it in place. 'You asked about this, and I told you T R, whoever he is, is my father. Caro and I are products of my mother's peccadillos. Moments she would like to pretend never occurred. However, when wailing children arrive nine months later, they are rather hard to hide. I suppose I should be glad the Marquis named me Framlington and did not leave me in a basket to die somewhere. But when I said I was an evil bastard, I truly am. Sins of the parents and all that.'

'Do not—'

'It is understandable,' he stopped her protest, 'that the Marquis hates me. What I have never been able to accept is that my mother hates me with equal wrath. I am a constant reminder of her shame, an embarrassment, nothing more, as is Caro. Their manner of resolving the issue is to ignore our existence.'

'I am sorry.' Mary unravelled from her self-protective pose.

'Why? It is not your fault, and I did not ask for your pity.'

She lay down beside him, mimicking his posture, her head on one palm as her free hand settled at his waist.

He closed his eyelids. 'If I see pity in your eyes, you will make me intensely angry again.'

'What about love? Can I look at you with love? It is not pity I am offering, it is love. If you are hurting, I hurt. I care. Is care allowed?'

Opening one eye, Drew gave her a crooked smile. Her eyes shone with concern, but mirth caught there too.

He opened his other eye and she laughed.

'Very well, I will accept care and raise it. I admit, I want to hate her, and I tell myself I hate her, and the rest of them – but I still desperately want to belong among them – and now you know I am not an evil bastard but a bitter unwanted child.'

'Not unwanted.'

Damn it. Her eyes glittered with pity. It pricked like a thorn in his side.

No. It is care. *Someone cares for me.* Warmth not anger stirred in his chest.

Mary threw away her buttercup and wrapped her hand about his, the one that still held the strand of grass. 'You are wanted.' She kissed the corner of his lips, then rolled onto her back and looked up at the sky.

She was so beautiful. He brushed the tip of the grass about her cheek and down her neck. 'But not by them; it is a hard lesson, well learned. I steel myself by saying I do not give a damn for their opinion, or anyone else's for that matter. But then I met you and I care for yours. You wished to meet them and for some ridiculous reason I thought perhaps, just perhaps, my mother would like you and be proud of me. I should not have taken you there.'

'You should have told me why you did not want to go. Had you said, I would not have persisted. The moment we walked in the door I knew it was wrong. But how could I have imagined that—'

'When your family all adore you.' He grazed the tip of the grass along the skin above her bodice. 'The Pembroke lions prowl and protect, preventing scandal or harm attacking their pride. Did you realise your womenfolk have been waging a subtle war against me, while your menfolk scowl?'

She smiled. 'You do not expect me to pity you for that, I hope? You chose to take them on.'

'And I have had my money's worth.'

'My money. And you chose to fight. Instead of making friends with them, you made them enemies.'

He dipped the tip of the grass into her cleavage, smiling. Pink stained her skin from her bodice upward. She was modest even now. A Pembroke to the heart. She would never cuckold him.

'Old habits die hard, darling. I do not trust people, especially families. I am judged by my birth and if the issue is their ignorance, why should I defend myself?'

'So now we are at the crux.' Her gaze gripped his. 'You do not like to be rejected, but you say you do not care and try to mask it.'

Drew threw away the piece of grass and instead picked a head of clover. 'I made up my mind, the afternoon you were ill and I saw how much I hurt you, that I was going to declare my love for you in your brother's drawing room.'

She laughed. 'Then, if they did not believe you, you would have told them all to go to hell.'

Drew laughed too. 'I suppose so...' He smiled wryly.

'Then my father would have told you to go to hell.'

'Careful, if you get a taste for foul language I will divorce you. You may like your men spirited. I like my women staid.' His gaze fell to the smile hovering on her lips as he placed the stem of the clover into her bodice and left the flower there. 'I do love you.'

When his gaze met hers, her emotions shone vividly for him to read, *I love you more than anything.* How long had he not seen that and hurt her regardless?

His hand cupped her breast over her bodice and he kissed her.

Her tongue played with his as her fingers combed into his hair.

He longed to lift her dress and take her here in the long grass.

But this was about building better foundations for them – they had never had a problem with their physical bond.

He ended the kiss, his mouth hovering just over hers. 'I will be different now.'

27

'I know you returned my dowry.'

His hazel eyes lost their rich amber depth and became shallow mirrors. He rolled on to his back, and raised one knee, his foot flat on the crushed grass as one arm slotted behind his head.

'As you said, it was your money. But I could not return the money I used to pay debts and support Caro.'

Mary rolled to her side, balanced her head on her palm and looked down at him.

'I do not regret rescuing Caro.' His eyes said, *damn the consequences.*

'I did not ask you to regret it; I would guess neither John nor Papa would either. They will think it heroic of you.' Her palm settled on his chest. Even through the fabric of his waistcoat, she could feel his heart beating.

'They will think me a sop. A man has a legal right to beat his wife if he chooses to, and they gave me the money to protect your security not Caro's.'

'I think you returning my dowry unbalanced John's opinion of you. He thought you without conscience, and then you did something that proved him wrong. He also thought you uncaring, but protecting your sister proves that wrong, too. He may have to like you now.'

'Except that I did once proposition his wife...' He smiled, wry amusement in his eyes.

Amusement lifted Mary's lips. 'Ah, yes, I forgot. You told me why, perhaps you could tell him. But that would mean admitting you care for his opinion.'

A smile parted his lips. 'Are you mocking me?'

'Perhaps. Why did you choose me over anyone else? If you were marrying for money in the beginning.'

His eyebrows lifted at the question and his smile fell. 'I told you. The first time I danced with you I knew. You were the most beautiful creature. But I remember you do not like to be appreciated for your looks. Yet that is the truth and you wanted honesty. It was more than that though. You danced with me, smiled and talked, as though I were any other man. You were charming. Perhaps I fell in love with you then. Certainly, I chose you then. The impulse was immediate and instinctive.'

'Except that during the waltz after that you asked Kate to share a bed with you. No more lies. I asked because I want to know the truth. Even if the truth is ugly, and merely because you liked my looks and money. I know it is not what you think now.'

His arm lifted from behind his head and his hand held hers against his heart. 'It is the truth. I asked your sister-in-law out of spite. I told you so. I am not proud of it. It is another of my faults. If people expect me to behave badly, I have an incontrollable itch to infuriate them. I did not know I had fallen in love moments before because I have never known love. All I knew was that I was mesmerised by you. When I saw you after that, a strange emptiness always gripped my stomach. I procrastinated, for a whole season. I needed money, you had it, and yet you seemed beyond any hope. But you kept glancing at me and you gave me hope.

'My bumping into you at that garden party was the only way I could think to speak to you, and when we met in that dark glasshouse my stomach was queasy with fear that you would reject me.' His eyes shone light brown, gilded with gold by the sunlight. 'But I should tell you the whole truth, I suppose…'

A frown creased Mary's brow.

'Since I danced with you the first night I met you, I have not bedded another woman. I may have said that to the Duchess, but since that night I have not wanted anyone but you. I wanted a monogamous marriage from the beginning, a love match. I wanted a faithful wife and to be a faithful husband.'

She slid her hand free and touched his cheek.

Andrew may have learned to love her, but he did not love himself. Probably because his parents had been so horrible.

He called himself an ass, she would call him wounded – but not aloud. 'And I chose to go out with your friend…' she said.

His eyebrows lifted. 'It was crass of me to judge you badly for that.' He caught hold of her fingers and kissed the tips. 'I knew it then, but I saw his hand on you and it triggered something. It was wrong of me.'

'In future may we always be honest with one another? I loved you from that first night too. You fascinated me. You were the only man there whenever you entered a room. I wish you had come forward and dealt openly with my father and told him the things you just told me, he would not have kept us apart. He always promised me my husband would be my choice. It is why John added to my dowry so my choice need not be restricted by a lack of money.'

'Your father would not have wanted a bastard for a son-in-law, especially not one with a rake's reputation.'

'My father will not care if you tell him you love me. He only wishes me happy – and you make me happy.'

He kissed her fingertips, then his breath hot on her skin, he said, 'I will tell him.'

She kissed his cheek. 'You are kind and he will see it,' she pressed a kiss on his brow, 'and good – when you wish to be.' She smiled. 'Yet most importantly you are mine and I love you, and I will never be unfaithful to you. Nor will I share you, Andrew.'

'When I took you away, when your father and your brother came to get you, I hated that you believed them and not me, and I was jealous of your love for them.'

'I was hurt by what they said because I love you. I did not want to believe what they said, but you did not say a single word to deny it.'

'My faults are legion. I shall apologise to your father.'

Mary kissed his lips, and said against them, 'I love you.'

His fingers splayed in her hair and he kissed her for a long while, their tongues dancing.

When they drew apart, she snuggled down, curled against him and rested her head on his shoulder, listening to the bees gathering honey from the clover.

Then she remembered, she had not been wholly honest with him yet. 'Andrew...'

'What, Mary?'

She lifted his hand to her stomach. 'This. You are to be a father. I am carrying your child.'

He sucked in a sharp breath of shock, and his hand lifted as he sat upright, leaving her to fall on her back on the grass, laughing.

'*God in heaven!* A child! Mary!'

His eyes shone like amber.

'Would you have told me if we were apart?'

Mary smiled. 'Yes. When I worked out how. Though, I would not have spoken with joy. But now we can be happy.'

'Our child…' His hand tentatively touched her stomach.

There was no visible change to her body, yet inside her a new life had been created. It was being nurtured.

'And we will love it,' she said.

Moisture glittered in his eyes, shifting emotions playing with his expressions, and tears ran onto his cheeks.

'We will be a family.' He smiled and wiped the tears away. 'Is there an earthquake somewhere? I feel as though the ground is rocking.' He looked into her eyes. 'I promise you, I will love our child and they will know everything good that I did not.'

She sat up. His words held the strength of vows.

'I feel as though something has broken inside me,' he said. 'It was hard, dark and cold. Now it is warm and light.'

He braced her face between his palms, wiped the tears from her cheeks with his thumbs, and kissed her fiercely.

A gong was struck, the sound ringing through the air. It announced that dinner was about to be served.

She pulled away. 'Oh goodness, do you think they have been waiting for us?' She stood. 'Do I look a state? Have I grass in my hair?'

'You look beautiful. Happy. Your cheeks have colour and your eyes are bright.'

He stood and offered her his hand to help her up.

'You cannot wear your coat.' She bent to pick it up. 'It is too creased. You must give it to John's valet to see if he can repair it.'

'I can live without it.' He took it from her hand.

'It is only John and Kate who know I am with child. I have not even told my mother and father.'

He smiled, wrapped an arm about her shoulders and pulled her close as they walked back to the house.

28

When Drew woke, Mary was fast asleep, so he left her in bed and walked to the lake to enjoy a cigar and absorb the quietness. It was calm here. Peaceful. When he returned, Mary had risen and gone to breakfast. He was on his way to join her.

Last night, the atmosphere during the evening meal had been strained. Pembroke, his duchess and Mary made polite conversation to avoid uncomfortable silence and the Duchess worked hard to draw him into it, but he had not really known what to say.

As soon as the meal was over, he escaped with Mary.

They retired to her rooms and talked for a long time, before falling asleep.

She woke him in the night, with a kiss. The kiss became urgent lovemaking in the utter darkness, serenaded by the calls of tawny owls through an open window. A warm breeze had brushed across his skin.

That was another special thing about this place, the air smelt clean; of the meadow grass and clover.

He woke her at dawn, and made love to her more slowly,

adoring every inch of her body. Afterwards she tucked herself beneath his arm and slept again.

Today, he knew, to the very depths of his marrow, that she was entirely his, and always would be.

'He does love me, John.'

Drew stopped midway across the hall at the sound of Mary's voice.

People who listened to conversations about themselves never heard anything good, Mary had learned that when she'd listened to his friends talking. And yet, he could not help it, he wanted to know what she said behind his back.

The door of the dining room was left open to a point that Drew could see the table was only occupied by Mary and her brother, and there were no servants in view.

Drew could see Mary's back and Pembroke looking at her.

'We watched you yesterday for a while, Katherine and I, when you were talking in the meadow. His behaviour certainly suggested he has feelings for you.'

'If you knew him...'

'He is not a man who is easily known.'

'But that does not make him bad, he has reasons to be wary.'

Her brother's gaze showed something Drew would not have recognised a few months ago – care. He cared immensely for his sister.

Pembroke smiled in a way Drew would not have thought him capable. Pembroke was different here at home.

Pembroke stood up.

Drew stepped back, trying to watch but not be seen.

'He promised to be different now.'

'I hope he is, for your sake, and I believe he has feelings for you. I wish you happy, as does Katherine.'

Drew took a bolstering breath and walked into the room. Now was his moment to prove Mary's words true. 'We will be happy.'

Suspicion glinted in Pembroke's eyes. He must wonder how much Drew had heard.

Enough to know that Pembroke was as close to Mary as Drew was to Caro.

Mary stood.

Drew walked to her side and held her hand. 'I love your sister, Pembroke, she will be happy.'

Pembroke smiled, with the mellow look Drew had only just discovered he was capable of.

'I shall leave you to your breakfast.' He nodded at Drew, then walked out.

Drew sat in a chair beside Mary.

'He approves. I told you he would. If you make me happy, Papa will approve too.'

29

Mary rested in the afternoon, leaving Drew at a loose end. They had explored more of the grounds on horseback before luncheon, but after luncheon, she said her condition had made her tired.

Drew also thought it might be because she had not been eating well. He had filled her plate at luncheon. But he did not want to disturb her sleep, so left her alone in bed.

He wandered along the upper hall, his hands in his pockets.

'Steady now, one step at a time.' Pembroke's deep tone had a happy sing-song pitch.

A gurgling, gleeful sound followed.

Drew saw Pembroke walking from the other direction, doubled over, his forefingers gripped by an infant's chubby little hands. The child toddled before Pembroke on unsteady feet, rocking and swaying, but grinning happily.

A lancing pain struck Drew in the chest.

He had eavesdropped this morning, but now he felt as if he were looking through a window and spying something so personal he should not see it.

Pembroke looked up and smiled. 'You have not met my son yet, have you?' He freed his fingers, held the child's waist, tossed him in the air and caught him, the child squealing. Then settled the boy's bottom on one forearm while protecting him from toppling with the other arm.

Drew felt as discombobulated as he had in Pembroke's drawing room in London.

'Katherine is lying down too. She is also expecting. Paul likes crawling on the short grass in the formal gardens, so I am taking him outside. Or rather he likes the endless space where there is nothing to make me say no. Are you going outside?'

'Yes.'

'Then we can keep each other company.'

Drew nodded. He followed Pembroke downstairs, while Pembroke crooned at the boy.

He tried to imagine himself with a child, but he could not.

When they reached the hall Pembroke ordered lemonade and cake to be served in the garden. They did not go out the front, but to the back, to the terrace, where the building gave some shade from the sun's rays.

Pembroke descended a flight of steps and put the child down on what Drew imagined was a croquet lawn, because it was perfectly flat, and scythed to half an inch in depth.

Watching the boy speed off on his hands and knees, Pembroke set his hands on his hips. 'It takes some time adjusting to fatherhood but it is magnificent. I shall never cease to wonder at the miracle of how a woman's body can create a child.'

Pembroke glanced at Drew. His expression said he understood that Drew was out of his depth and treading water hard, trying not to sink.

'You may practise getting to know children with my son, if you wish, or dive into the deep when your own arrives.'

The expression in Pembroke's eyes implied he was laughing at Drew, without actually laughing. 'I was like you,' he said. 'But you know that. I did not think I could love. I assure you, when the child arrives you will have no choice but to love him or her. You will be smitten at first sight. You are not like your parents, any more than I was like my grandfather. You will love the child.'

Drew's hand combed through his hair, hiding how much his hand shook.

The servants delivered the lemonade and Pembroke ran to fetch the boy who had reached the edge of the lawn.

They sat on the terrace while Pembroke fed his son pieces of cake and sips of lemonade. Drew smoked a cigar, mesmerised by them, wanting to learn how to be the same. He would cherish his children.

When the cake had all gone, Drew and Pembroke sat on the steps to watch the boy crawl over the grass.

'I have a property you may be interested in,' Pembroke said. 'It is on the edge of my estate, a few miles away, so you would not literally be on my doorstep. It is a small manor, with income from two tenanted farms which are part of the property, and a home farm. I will give you Mary's dowry back, so, I would expect you to purchase the manor and lands, but at a fair rate. Or I could lease it to you, but in that case you would not have the chance to pass it on to your child in future years.'

'And you fancy having us close,' Drew quipped. 'So you can keep an eye on me, and Mary, because you do not trust me.'

Pembroke held Drew's gaze, but there was no fierceness or challenge in his expression.

'I do not wish you close, but I wish Mary happy and settled. The property is ideal. You and I were acquaintances once, perhaps if you let down your guard, we could be friends. Certainly, Mary would like to have Kate and I near.'

And Mary was the most important thing to them all.

'You may show me this manor, and I will consider it.'

'We can ride there tomorrow.'

30

Andrew had been solicitous every day since he arrived here. They rode horses about the grounds, talked and walked, and in the evenings, they played cards with Kate and John, or Andrew read a book to her, or he sat beside her and turned the music as she played the pianoforte and sang.

He was purchasing a property from John. It was nestled in woodland, halfway down a hill which dropped into a river valley. An old Tudor manor, with wooden beams forming a skeleton through red bricks. It was not large, but it was charming.

The house was his favourite topic of conversation. He talked about making it a home, and he was already learning about farming and estate management from John and his steward. One afternoon, he had ridden out to the farms that would become his and met the tenants and labourers.

Now, he was sitting in a chair that caught the sunlight from a long window, reading a newspaper, his shoulders relaxed and a smile on his lips. The Andrew she knew visible to John and Kate too.

Mary looked up from her needlework as a footman hurried into the room. He said something to Finch who then spoke up. 'A carriage is approaching, Your Grace.'

John had Paul on his knee. He looked at the footman. 'Is there a coat of arms on it?'

'There is, Your Grace.'

John stood, lifting Paul to his hip. 'Well, it appears we have a guest. Finch, would you ask the kitchen to be prepared and send for the nursery maid? I will go downstairs. Katherine, would you hold Paul until the maid comes?'

Andrew stood too. 'May I join you?' Mary knew he was wary of Lord Kilbride's threats.

She put down her sewing and stood too, as John passed Paul to Katherine. 'I shall come with you.'

John walked to the window as they heard the carriage and horses on the gravel near the house.

'It is Uncle Richard's insignia.'

Mary looked at Andrew, thinking what he was probably thinking – that her uncle would have news from London.

A few moments later, she walked across the gravel outside, as a footman put down the carriage step.

Richard climbed down. 'John.' Richard's voice rang deep with formality. He looked at Andrew.

Mary held Andrew's hand, knowing he would face another test.

'How are things?' Uncle Richard asked John.

'Well,' John answered.

'Things are fine, Your Grace,' Andrew said, as though he thought the question was code for *and how do you find Lord Framlington...* 'Have you come all this way to ask that?'

John glanced across his shoulder, his expression asking Andrew for restraint. 'Things are fine,' he said to Uncle Richard.

'When a certain person knows when to restrain his bravado. What has brought you here?'

'I need to speak to Lord Framlington. May we go inside?'

Mary knew John had written to Uncle Richard and told him Andrew was here, and that he was innocent. Her uncle had not replied, and his expression said he did not trust John's judgement.

Andrew's fingers wrapped more firmly around her hand. He need not worry, she would not leave him to face this alone.

'We will go up to the family drawing room,' Kate said, from behind them. 'I asked the kitchen to send up a tea tray.'

Uncle Richard lifted a hand, encouraging Andrew to lead the way.

Mary's heart pounded.

What was this?

What new disaster?

In the drawing room, she sat, before she fell down, her legs were so wobbly. Andrew stood behind the chair, his palms resting on her shoulders.

Uncle Richard did not sit either. Nor did John.

'What is it?' Andrew asked, his voice a deep concerned pitch. 'What charge have you against me now?'

'It is a formal charge – of incest. I came to take you back to London. If the story you told Mary and John is true, then you must tell it to a magistrate. Your only other option is to flee the country, and I will not have that, for Mary's sake. You must ask your sister to speak to the magistrate too.'

'I will come with you, but I am not giving Kilbride a chance to catch Caro.'

'You would face one man's word against another, then, and you will risk hanging. All the evidence points to one conclusion. You at least need your sister to deny the accusation too.'

Andrew's breath released as a sigh. 'I will risk hanging

anyway; her word may count for nothing, as I am sure you know, and I will not risk her.'

Mary's hands touched those on her shoulders, as she looked up at him. 'Andrew.' Her voice begged him to do whatever her uncle asked.

'I cannot do it,' he told her. 'I hid her alone; she has no one to protect her. If she came out of hiding and they did not believe either of us, Kilbride *will* kill her. I am happy to go with you, but I will not betray Caro. She is safe only as long as no one knows where she is.'

'Lady Kilbride may come here,' John said. 'If you go to London, Andrew, I will fetch her. She can live here for as long as she wishes. You know she will be safe; you have seen how many servants I have. They can protect her. No one can come to the house without their knowing.'

Andrew hesitated. Mary was not sure he trusted John enough.

'It is a good idea,' her uncle said. 'I am sure the magistrate would speak to her here, and Lady Kilbride would be safe whatever the outcome. Remember, this allegation is raised against her also.'

Andrew still did not agree, his eyes a deep sea of thoughts.

'You trust me,' she told him quietly. 'I will go with John and persuade your sister to come here. She will be safe, and then she can speak for you.'

He let out a slow breath that sought to manage his emotions. 'Very well, bring her here. I will give Mary the address and a letter from me, so she will know she is safe with you. But you must be watchful, John. She will be in danger.'

There was a knock at the drawing room door. 'Tea, Your Grace.'

As Uncle Richard and John drank tea and ate cake with

Katherine, Mary took Andrew up to her room to write his letter. He wrote the letter in front of her, in the script she knew. His friends might have come up with the words in his letters but he had written them.

When he finished, he blotted the ink, folded the paper and handed it to her.

'It is addressed,' he said. 'Keep it safe.'

'I will.'

He held her hand. 'I hope this will be settled quickly. I should go now; the sooner I go, the sooner I will return.' His smile offered reassurances he could not give.

She nodded, biting the tip of her tongue, trying not to cry, because tears would not help him. She must be strong for him.

'Come on.'

He held her hand as they walked downstairs to the first-floor drawing room.

'Framlington,' her uncle said, acknowledging Andrew as they entered the room.

'I am ready,' Andrew said.

Ten minutes later, she stood on the steps beneath the massive stone portico, holding Andrew, his forehead resting against hers.

'Goodbye,' Mary said, her tears refusing to be restrained.

John and Kate stood beside them. Uncle Richard was waiting in the carriage.

Andrew wiped away her tears with his thumbs and kissed her fiercely for a short time. 'I am coming back,' he said. 'I am sorry I dragged you into this muddle, but I do not regret helping Caro.'

'I am glad you helped her. I love you.'

'I love you too,' he whispered back and kissed her again. 'Goodbye,' he said as he released her. Then he walked away and climbed into the carriage.

A footman closed the door.

He waved from the window as it pulled away. She held her hand high and waved until she could no longer see the carriage.

'We should fetch Lady Kilbride immediately,' John said.

31

When the carriage drove into Maidstone, John looked at her. 'Where are we to go then, Mary?'

Andrew's letter was tucked into her bodice against her skin. She had told John they must go to Maidstone, but nothing else. Her fingers shaking, Mary pulled out the letter from beneath her clothes and showed John the address. 'Please check no one has followed us. Lord Kilbride might have had someone waiting outside your gates.'

'He did not. The grooms checked.'

They had travelled in an old, unmarked carriage, and the grooms were dressed in their own clothing not John's livery.

John slid open the hatch in order to speak to the driver. 'Please stop at the next inn you see. Thank you.' He closed the hatch.

'We will walk from there,' he said to Mary.

It was only a few minutes before the carriage driver steered the horses through an arch into the stable yard of an inn. When it stopped, John opened the door, climbed down, then helped Mary alight.

'Come,' he said quietly, ignoring his staff, as they ignored him, as though he were not a duke.

She lay her hand on his arm.

They walked past the Bishop's Palace, and the ford beside it, to find the row of terraced cottages Andrew had described to her.

Most of the narrow front gardens were planted with vegetables, apart from one; Caroline's was planted with flowers, hollyhocks, delphiniums, and frail flowers which looked like tiny bonnets. The garden was just as Andrew had described.

'Wait here,' she told John. 'Lady Kilbride may not open the door if she sees a gentleman calling.'

'Indeed.' John nodded.

He waited at the end of the row of cottages. She walked on. She opened the low gate and walked along a narrow brick paved path to the front door.

The oak door was as squat as the thatched cottage.

Mary dropped the knocker against the door four times, the low thuds vibrating through the wood.

There was no answer.

But beyond the door Mary heard whispers.

She waited.

'Who is there?' an older woman's voice called.

Mary leaned close to the door. 'It is your sister-in-law,' she said quietly. 'Your brother sent me because he could not come himself.'

Another hushed, urgent conversation ensued on the other side of the door.

Then bolts clunked back, the door opened an inch and an older woman, Mary presumed to be the housekeeper, peered through the gap. She wore a black dress, dusted with flour, as though she had been interrupted at work in the kitchen and had stripped off an apron a moment ago.

'May I come in?' Mary asked.

The door opened a little wider. Beyond the housekeeper, Mary saw Lady Kilbride standing in the shadows of a small room. She had a brown woollen shawl wrapped tightly about her. Her dress beneath it looked plain, homely, and her hair was simply coiled and pinned in a knot. She must have lived extravagantly previously, but now she had been living humbly.

'May I come in?' Mary said again. 'My brother, the Duke of Pembroke, is with me. Andrew sent us both.'

Lady Kilbride's gaze reached past Mary, appearing afraid.

Mary held out the letter. 'I have this from Andrew, so you know I am telling you the truth.'

Lady Kilbride took the letter and opened it.

Mary glanced back and beckoned John forward.

As she read, the colour in Lady Kilbride's skin faded. 'He has accused Drew of being my lover. I never thought... *Oh God.*' Her hand rested against her chest. 'Come in. Before someone sees you.' She stepped back, beckoning them in. 'You are too well dressed to visit a simple woman.'

Mary crossed the threshold onto stone flags. The room was a parlour, a third of the size of the room in The Albany.

Lady Kilbride's eyes looked past Mary as John entered behind her, removing his hat and bending his head to pass beneath the low lintel. 'Your Grace,' she said. 'You must sit.' She lifted a hand towards one of two armchairs in the room.

'Drew must regret helping me,' she said.

'Ma'am, sit down before you fall down,' the housekeeper encouraged. 'I shall make a pot of tea.'

Mary smiled as she imagined Andrew employing this woman. She sounded like someone who would defend her mistress, even with violence if necessary. 'Helping you is the one thing he would never regret,' Mary said as Lady Kilbride sat in the other armchair.

Mary turned a chair from a table in the corner and occupied that.

The letter quivered in Lady Kilbride's trembling hands.

'I promised your brother I would protect you in his stead,' John said. 'You will be safe at Pembroke Place. No one can come within a mile of the house without being seen. We will be there to keep you company. Of course, the house and grounds will be at your disposal to use as you wish, you may avoid us all if you choose. But it need not be confinement as this must feel, and you need not live in fear.'

'Why would you help me?'

Mary remembered Andrew's poisonous family. They were Lady Kilbride's family too. 'Because you are my sister now.'

'You are together?' Her eyes were very like Andrew's. Like their mother's, Mary supposed.

'Yes.'

'He deserves to be happy.'

'I think so too.'

'He is a good man,' Lady Kilbride said as though Mary needed to be convinced. 'I owe him so much.'

'Will you come with us?' John asked.

Lady Kilbride nodded. 'I will.'

'Then we should go directly.' Mary stood. 'John can send a cart back for your possessions.'

'I have only one bag. I left my husband with nothing.'

32

As Drew stood before the magistrate, accounting for his actions, the Duke of Arundel sat nearby watching and listening, with a face like stone. The pompous man who quizzed Drew grunted at his answers and scowled as he spoke, while a clerk scribbled every word on a roll of paper. Drew did not think he was convincing any of them of his innocence. The world believed too deeply in the reputation his birth had given him.

But incest... That was a hideous charge.

Drew's stomach roiled as he fought anger and frustration. It disgusted him that people would think him so low.

His only counter was that he had been protecting Caro. *But there is no law against a man beating his wife – and how the hell do I prove I have not had intercourse with my sister?*

Hatred burned in his veins as he walked from the court to await an intermediate verdict on his fate. Where were his mother and brothers who should be denying this? The Duke of Arundel was the only one who sat beside Drew on the hard wooden bench outside the court room. Mary's family, not his.

Drew's elbows rested on his knees, his head held in his hands.

Fear bit into his innards as he thought of Caro. *Where was she now? What would this mean for her?*

'Lord Framlington!' His name echoed about the stone hall. 'Please come with me.'

As Drew stood, he met Wiltshire's gaze. His expression did not say he believed Drew's fate would be positive.

In the dark wood-panelled courtroom, he stood before the magistrate again.

'Lord Framlington, you will be held in custody until I have spoken with Lady Kilbride.'

Drew bit his tongue. He feared that Kilbride had influence over this man and he would use this to find Caro.

'You will tell the clerk Lady Kilbride's address. Lord Kilbride has assured me you know it.'

Drew's back stiffened. 'If you think I will give my sister into Kilbride's hands, you may—'

'Lord Framlington!' Wiltshire stood. 'Have sense. Unless you wish a noose about your neck then you must agree, and I do not want to see my niece a widow when she is barely wed. Lady Kilbride is safe with John, tell them.'

Damn it. 'I shall give you my sister's address, sir, if you agree to the Duke of Arundel accompanying you and remaining present while she is questioned. Then I will be sure she is neither threatened nor coerced.'

'I will ensure it,' Wiltshire agreed. Yet it was not his decision.

The weight of a Duke's voice exceeded any bar royalty, though.

'Agreed,' the magistrate said.

Wiltshire was a principled man, Drew trusted him.

Before Wiltshire left, he paid the prison officer, acquiring a solitary cell for Drew, with sheets on his bed and the provision of decent, if not nice, meals.

'Thank you,' Drew said. 'Please tell Mary I love her.'

'I will tell her I am doing my utmost to get you home to her.'

Drew had done nothing to deserve this man's help, and yet he was helping him. This was the family who loved Mary.

'Tell John to make sure she eats. She has a habit of not eating when she is distressed and she must think of the child.'

'The child?' Wiltshire's eyebrows rose.

Andrew simply looked at him. What was there to say?

Wiltshire's hand rested on Drew's shoulder. 'We will get you out of this.'

When he left, the key turned in the cell door, locking Drew in. The cell was private but it was probably only a yard and a half wide, and two yards long, and the grey stone was gloomy, slimy with damp and cold.

He hated silence and solitude; it encouraged introspection and he had always avoided that.

He lay down on the narrow bunk, with its uncomfortable straw mattress, shut his eyes and tried to sleep.

Sleep would be better than being alone with his thoughts.

33

Drew paced the length of the cell, sat for a while, then paced again. He would hear nothing today. The magistrate would ride out to John's and speak with Caro.

At midday, he heard the sound of keys jangling and footsteps walking along the hall.

He went to the small square of bars in the door and strained to look through them.

The guard was followed by Peter.

Drew's hands wrapped around the cold metal bars and he smiled as Peter came close.

The guard lifted the key to the lock and Drew stepped back, to let the door open.

Peter walked in and threw a newspaper and a small tin of cigars onto Drew's narrow mattress, as the guard shut and locked the door behind him.

Drew sat down. 'Feel free to claim a seat...' he told Peter.

Hands in his pockets, Peter looked down. 'If it has fleas I will decline.'

A humorous sound broke from the back of Drew's throat. 'If it has fleas then so do I.'

'Mark and Harry are with me, but they would only let one of us up here.'

Drew met Peter's gaze. 'It is a sorry ending, is it not?'

'I doubt it is the end.' Peter moved the newspaper aside and sat among the fleas. 'You are a part of the Pembrokes' clan now, my friend. They are like a damned army, sweeping through every ballroom and salon dispelling the rumours. Someone mentions your name and one of them is there, putting them straight. Uncles, aunts, cousins, cousins of cousins... Marrying Mary was the best thing you could have done.'

'It was.' But not for that reason.

Peter slapped a hand on his shoulder. 'When you get out of here, now you have such powerful friends, you will no longer want to know us.'

'You will always be my friend.'

'Mary may not like that.'

'Mary will not mind. Things are good between us again.'

'I am glad for you then.'

'I am to be a father.'

'I'll be damned. Though I suppose it was inevitable. Poor child,' Peter joked.

Amusement choked from Drew's throat. 'If I get out of here, just for your humour, and because I could not have you as my groom's man, I shall make you godfather, and if I do not get out of here, you must tell Mary it is what I wished. The child will be in the cradle of her family, but my child ought to have some memory of me.'

'Should I share tales of you in your cups?'

Drew did not laugh this time.

Peter's hand settled on Drew's shoulder. 'You have Pembroke's and Wiltshire's influence, you will get out.'

'I am not certain. Kilbride has influence too.'

'Enough!' The guard shouted through the square opening in the door, announcing that Peter's allotted time was up.

34

Mary leaned against the drawing room door, her ear pressed to the wood, trying to hear what was being said. But Caroline spoke too quietly.

Mary looked at John. 'I cannot hear.'

'You should not be listening.'

'What if the magistrate does not believe Caroline?'

'Then he is an idiot. The accusation is obviously not true.'

Mary had been resolute since they fetched Caroline, suppressing her fear for Andrew, facing this with courage, refusing to think they might believe Drew guilty. But... No... She could not consider it.

'I sent a letter to Mama and asked them to come, Mary. I think you need her here.'

'Do you think Richard will take me back to London with him, so I can see Andrew?'

John shook his head. 'No. I doubt, with the amount of pride your husband has, he would thank us for letting you see him in such a situation. Stay here and support Lady Kilbride. That is how you may help. You are the only person she trusts. Let Uncle Richard manage this and speak for Andrew.'

But only the words Caroline spoke on the other side of the door might bring him back.

The door handle turned. Mary stepped back, as Uncle Richard opened the door.

He looked from Mary to John. 'We have finished, and I believe Lady Kilbride would appreciate your company, Mary. John, may I dine here before I return to town?'

'Of course,' John answered.

Leaving John to play the obsequious role to influence the magistrate, Mary hurried to Caroline.

She was shaking terribly.

'I am sorry you had to endure this.' Mary slipped off her shawl and wrapped it around Caroline's shoulders.

'Better that than for Drew to suffer because of me.' Her eyes swam with tears.

Mary held her, tears filling her eyes too, and for a short while they clung to each other.

Caroline broke the embrace. 'I am sorry. I do not normally cry.'

Mary wiped her eyes and smiled. 'I do, and there is no need to apologise.'

'This is my fault,' Caroline said.

'It is no one's fault but your husband's. We must remain confident and trust my Uncle Richard to return Andrew to us.'

'The magistrate did not trust my word. He is going to speak with one of my lady's maids and ask her to confirm what I said. The whole thing is mortifying. Embarrassing. Then I think of Drew in a cell, alone. He did nothing to deserve this.'

'I know. And we must have faith that the truth becomes known.'

'Thank you for helping us, Mary. Drew needed a woman like you.'

'And I needed a man like him.' Mary smiled.

A light knock struck the door, which John had left ajar. 'Come in!' Mary called.

'Sorry to interrupt.' It was Kate. 'We are serving dinner. Your uncle is staying with us to dine, Mary, and he sent me to fetch you. Will you dine with us, Lady Kilbride?'

Caroline shook her head. 'May I eat in my room? I am too tired to converse.'

'Of course,' Kate said. 'I will ask for your meal to be sent up.'

'I shall be there in a moment,' Mary said, encouraging Kate to leave them alone again.

'I am sorry,' Caroline whispered after Kate left. 'They must think me rude.'

'John and Kate will not mind if you keep to your room. You must not feel pressed to be in our company and do as you please. If you need to speak to me, send a servant to find me.'

'Thank you.'

35

Another visitor arrived as day became dusk. Drew stood as the key turned in the lock of the cell's door.

The door opened.

The Duke of Arundel entered. He did not smile.

The door shut, and locked.

'Do you have news?' Drew asked.

'Not yet.'

Drew sat, because there was too little room for them both to stand. Wiltshire remained on his feet.

'Lady Kilbride has confirmed everything you said. But the magistrate is conscious it could just be lies that the two of you have made up—'

'It is not li—'

'I have not finished.' Wiltshire lifted a staying hand. 'The magistrate intends to speak with a former lady's maid, who could provide evidence on whether or not the beatings took place. If she confirms she saw the beatings and bruises, then the magistrate has said he is willing to accept the charge is not true.'

'Did you see Mary? How is she? How is Caro?'

'Mary sends her love to you, and your sister is a strong woman, she will cope. We will not see her suffer. Yet she is frightened. She did not want to tell her story, she did so to help you. She is more frightened for you than she is for herself. But I promise you, whatever happens I will not let her be harmed in any way.'

'Thank you.'

'I also spoke to your father.'

Drew stood, astonished and instantly irate. His hands curled to fists. 'You did not speak to my father, Your Grace. That is impossible because I have no idea who the hell he is.'

'So I discovered,' Wiltshire answered, not reacting to Drew's anger, yet not showing regret either. '*Is* Lady Kilbride your sister?'

Drew's eyes narrowed. 'If you hope to get me off on those grounds, you cannot. Caro and I share a mother, but the Marquis is not our father.'

'I see. I only asked because I know some families take illegitimate children from other mothers too.'

He did not see, he would have no concept of it, no more of a concept than Mary had. But now he knew just how low a match his niece had made. 'You could, of course, leave me to hang. You would be rid of me then.'

Wiltshire's eyebrows lifted. 'You think I think less of you because of your parentage. I do not judge a man by his birth, I judge him by his actions, Lord Framlington. I judged you as a bad man, when you ran off with my niece. I judged you even worse when you hit Lord Brooke in a public place. And I admit, when I first heard this accusation, I thought you the lowest of scum.

'But now I know the truth. You helped your sister, not harmed her, and I have seen how Lord Brooke respects you despite that brawl, but most importantly I know of your true affections for my niece. I judge facts, and so now I know the truth I am doing my utmost to get you out of this mess and I will continue to do so. But I can tell you, neither you nor Lady Kilbride will have any help from your family.'

'Pray tell me something I do not know.'

Wiltshire held Drew's shoulder. 'It is of no matter, you are part of Mary's family now.'

Devil take it. Emotion caught in Drew's throat and punched him in the chest. This was what he had craved when he watched Mary in the beginning – to be a part of a family like hers. He had hoped to steal her away and make their own family. He had never considered he might become a part of her life like this.

'I am grateful, Your Grace.' No more words would come without displaying the emotions he would rather hide.

'Not Your Grace, just Richard.' Wiltshire's grip on Drew's shoulder firmed. 'You are my nephew now.'

'Enough!' The shout came from outside.

'Keep your chin up,' Wiltshire said as the guard let him out.

When the door shut, Drew sat down, wondering if he got out of here, how he would fit into the heart of Mary's family when he had struggled on the edges.

36

The sun's light crept across the grey stone in the cell as the sun breached the horizon. Another day of incarceration dawning. Drew sighed. He was bored of lying on an uncomfortable mattress, staring at the same four walls.

How people survived years in prisons he had no clue. The hours of the day were marked only by the jangle of keys.

The first jangle came when a lump of dry bread was handed to him through the bars.

The second came an hour after that... Too early for luncheon.

Drew stood and looked through the hole in the door trying to see if someone was coming to visit him.

Peter smiled at him from behind the jailor's shoulder.

Drew stepped back as the door was unlocked.

'You will not believe this...' Peter began, with a broad grin, when the jailor closed the door. 'Wiltshire confronted Kilbride last night. It was deliberately done to be a spectacle. He challenged him in the middle of the Devonshires' ballroom, raising his voice so all could hear and denouncing Kilbride's claims as an utter lie. When Kilbride argued, Wiltshire turned to the crowd and told them they would hear the truth in the morning.'

'Those were bold words.' Drew rubbed his unshaven jaw. 'I am not so convinced. It is still the word of a bastard against that of a nobleman.'

Peter risked the fleas again and sat on the mattress. 'Not now. Now it is the word of twenty noblemen, as well as you and Caro, against a single man. They were all there, Mary's uncles and cousins, standing behind Wiltshire, ready to defend you and Caro. When Wiltshire was done, the room was abuzz with women claiming you must be the wounded party. People trust that family, and if that family is on your side – they trust you. Harry and Mark are bragging about being your friends.'

'To win women.'

'To win women,' Peter agreed, and laughed.

Drew shook his head, a shallow smile raising his lips.

'Your mother and the Marquis were there,' Peter added. 'They walked out.'

'Please tell me Wiltshire did not threaten them too?'

'No, but he scowled.' Peter grinned.

Drew grimaced. 'I have had enough of this place.'

'By the end of the day, you will be out of here.'

'I wish I was sure.'

'I am sure. That is enough. Do you think Pembroke will mind if I call on you at his estate?'

'I doubt he would turn you away.'

'Good enough. I will call on you in a day or two.'

'Enough!'

'I am sick of that man's voice ordering my day,' Drew whispered bitterly.

'It will be over soon.' Peter slapped Drew's shoulder.

'Please God you are right.'

* * *

When the keys jangled for the fourth time that day, Drew did not get up. It would be the evening meal, and surely then too late for any word from the magistrate.

'Stand up, Lord Framlington.' It was not the guard who spoke.

Drew's heart pounded as the door opened wider. Then he saw Richard behind the stranger.

'You are cleared of the charge and free to go. Here.' The stranger held out a roll of paper, which Drew presumed confirmed the magistrate's verdict.

Drew grasped it, not that he needed a piece of paper to tell him he had done nothing wrong.

Wiltshire held out a hand and shook Drew's firmly.

'Thank you.' Drew spoke before he could.

'You are welcome,' he answered. 'Now, let us get you back to Mary.'

Drew jogged down the stone steps ahead of Wiltshire, eager to get out. A man opened the prison door.

The light blinded Drew for a moment. He had never felt so happy to see the sun.

'You could stay with me tonight, so you can shave and such. I will run you out to Pembroke Place in the morning. Or we can leave now and we might make it before dusk.'

'I want to go now, to see Mary.'

'Then we leave now. The numbers have grown at Pembroke Place, though, the family are gathering.'

Drew's heart pounded hard. He wanted to see Mary but he did not welcome the trial of meeting her entire family again.

They drove out of London during the fashionable, crowded hour, which made the journey slower and tedious. Some people sought to peer into the carriage, as if they thought Drew might be inside. He pulled down the blind.

Wiltshire laughed.

When the carriage stopped again, Drew's natural impatience rose. He itched to leap from the carriage and run to Pembroke's, not that that would get him to Mary any faster.

Wiltshire touched Drew's arm. 'We will get there, lad, however long it takes. Cool your temper and learn to consider the consequences before you let it rise.'

Drew moved his arm. 'I am grateful for all you have done, Richard. But do not tell me what I should or should not do.'

'Lord Framlington, I think that is something you have lacked. From what I have seen, you had no one to guide you appropriately. I cannot tell you what to do, no, but I can and will advise you. You may choose whether to listen.'

Drew sneered, but even so... 'Please call me Drew.'

'Yet, Mary calls you Andrew.'

'Because I was fool enough to tell her it was my given name, and now she insists on it to recognise all that I am, and not the man other people see.'

'I am getting to know you, Drew. You are aggressive only when you feel threatened. I am no threat, and nor is anyone else in Mary's family. But put up your guard and it will take thrice as long for you to feel welcome.' Honouring his word, he said no more, leaving Drew to consider if he should heed Richard's advice, or not.

Drew pulled down the brim of his hat, slid down in the seat and rested a boot heel on the far side.

Richard laughed.

Drew smiled to himself, shaking his head over the knowledge that his behaviour had become a thing of amusement.

37

Mary hovered on the first-floor landing, her fingers on the banister as she watched the hall below.

Laughter rang from the downstairs drawing room, echoing about the marble and plaster sculpting. The house was full. John had sent for her mother and father, which meant her sisters and brothers had come too. Then everyone had come from London today, after Uncle Richard had challenged the Marquis of Kilbride. They thought she and Caroline would welcome their support. They did not realise poor Caroline would be embarrassed. She was mortified to think that London knew so much about her marriage. She had not come out of her room since everyone arrived, and she had also declined Mary's company.

Mary did not want to go into the drawing room either. Everyone was discussing the part they had played last night, and how exciting it was to see a villain stumbling for words. Everyone believed Andrew innocent, and everyone told her they were happy he had proved them wrong.

But all the well-wishing and self-congratulation was irrelevant. *He is not here!*

People believed Andrew would be freed today. Yet, there was no surety.

She could not sit among them and listen to chatter and laughter, when inside she was still scared for him.

She stared at the front door, willing Andrew to walk through it.

Another round of laughter echoed from the formal drawing room.

Mary pushed away from the banister and went downstairs. She had to get out of this house.

A footman appeared when she reached the hall. 'If anyone asks where I am,' she said, 'please say I am walking in the park.'

She slipped out the front door, without a bonnet or shawl. The day was warm, and the sun might damage her skin, but she did not care. Outside, her feet led her along the gravel drive. Her arms clutched across her chest.

She walked past the stables.

It was nearly six. Surely if Andrew was coming today, he would be here soon.

Her arms uncrossed and fell to her sides, as her pace quickened, walking along the drive towards the distant gates.

Perhaps he was on his way. Perhaps he was near.

She ran, in an unladylike manner, as quickly as she had done as a girl, with the hem of the skirt of her dress rising above her knees.

If she could grow wings, she would fly to him.

She ran until a stitch in her side stopped her, then she walked, with a hand pressed to her side.

John's drive went on forever, she could not see the entrance gates yet.

When the stitch eased, she ran again, until the gates and gate house were in sight. She slowed a hundred yards from them. She did not want the gatekeeper to see her this far from the house; she was not dressed for the outdoors.

She clutched her arms across her chest and looked at the gates, waiting.

38

When the carriage turned through the gates of Pembroke's estate, Drew sat up straight, lifting off his hat so he could lean his head against the window and see ahead.

A lone woman stood by the side of the drive a few yards away. She was far away from the house.

He pulled the window strap, to pull the glass down. Throwing his hat on the far seat, he leaned out.

'Mary!'

Her hand lifted.

He ducked back in and knocked on the carriage roof urgently, telling the driver to stop.

'What is it?' Wiltshire asked.

A lopsided smile tugged Andrew's lips as he looked over his shoulder. 'Your niece, the daft girl. Heaven knows what she is doing right out here?'

Love, a painful but beautiful ache, ran through his blood. Drew turned the door latch as the carriage stopped, leapt out and ran the few paces to her as she ran at him too. He caught her up off her feet and twirled her around, as her arms embraced his neck. When he set her on her feet, they kissed.

He could grow to like these homecomings too much. The feeling was addictive.

Tears made her eyes appear like glass, and her palms braced his unshaven jaw.

'I smell like a sewer and look like a vagrant, I know,' he said. 'But I did not want to waste a minute getting back to you.'

'I feared they would not let you go.'

'They would not have done, had not your uncle become involved. I am in debt to him.'

'I thought I had lost you,' she said.

'No, and not ever now. What are you doing this far from the house?'

'I walked out to wait for you, in the hope you would come.'

'Mary! Drew! Are you getting into the carriage?' Richard called.

'Yes! Hello, Uncle Richard!' Mary called back.

Drew tucked Mary protectively beneath his arm as they walked to the carriage. 'Your uncle told me the house is full of your family. Is there a way we can avoid them for now?'

'If the carriage goes into the stable yard we can enter the house through the servants' hall.'

'Then that is what we will do.'

39

Mary was sitting on the bed, her knees bent up and clasped by her arms, her stockinged feet balancing on the very edge of the mattress, toes peeping from beneath the hem of her dress.

'You look charming, my love.' Andrew's head rested on the back of the copper tub. 'Why not get into the water with me?' He deployed his roguish smile.

'When my entire family would be guessing why I was late for dinner. Thank you, I shall resist.'

'We could eat up here.'

'You have just won their favour; do not antagonise them now.'

He sat upright, then stood, the water streaming down his naked body. 'So, I escaped jail, but I am sentenced to their company.'

'You are.' She smiled, knowing his nakedness was another ploy to win her over. Her eyes followed his movement, her heart longing to give in.

'Why can we not dally here? We could lie on the bed and feed each other in the way of ancient Romans.'

'Or...' She uncurled her legs and slid from the bed, smiling at him as she reached for the towel and threw it at him. 'You could stop procrastinating and dress. Then we can go down to dinner.'

He caught the towel.

'Just remember, Andrew, I am on to you now. No shocking my family and hiding behind deviltry. I want them to know you.'

Laughter was his answer as he rubbed the towel across his chest.

When they eventually progressed to dinner, the smooth satin of Mary's dress caressed her skin, in a way that made her feel both beautiful and elegant.

'You look gorgeous, by the way,' Andrew whispered through the edge of his lips, his eyes on the footmen in the hall below.

When he offered his arm to her before they left the room, he said, 'You may take me to my sentence.'

'It is not a sentence. Please do not upset them,' she had chided.

'I will behave, Mary, I promise, no nonsense.'

Despite his promise, her heart beat in a firm, fearful pace as she heard the hum of conversation.

'How many are here?' he asked.

'All my uncles and aunts and their families, and my older cousins with their husbands. The younger children are in the nursery, but the older children will be dining with us. The boys are back from college.'

'We are speaking of a horde then, and your father?'

'Of course.'

Andrew stopped halfway down the stairs and took a deep breath.

'Andrew?'

He took another breath, and sighed it out, then lifted her hand from his coat sleeve. 'You asked me to show you how I feel. This is how I feel right now.' He pressed her hand to his chest,

over his heart. She could feel the pulse even through his waistcoat and her glove.

She smiled reassuringly. 'If you are nice to them, they will be
nice to you.'

'I think I should speak to your father alone first. If I go to the
library would you fetch him?'

'Why?'

'Because I need to put things straight, sweetheart.'

40

Drew had been waiting alone in Pembroke's opulent library for ten excruciating minutes. He wiped his damp palms on the front of his waistcoat. He held his hands together behind his back and stared up at a portrait of John's Duchess, her hair was half up and half down, and her shoulder turned to the room, showing a perspective that made her look like any other woman.

The door handle turned. Drew's heart pounded.

'Mary said you asked to speak with me, Framlington?' Marlow did not look pleased about it. 'You do realise you are keeping us all away from the dinner table.'

Drew sucked in a deep breath. Humble pie had a bitter taste. 'Lord Marlow, may I ask you for Mary's hand in marriage.'

The man looked at him askance. 'It is a little late, don't you think?'

Drew sighed. 'Yes, sir, I know, but I did not ask, and now I wish to rectify the matter.'

Marlow's arms folded over his chest. 'What folly, what game is this, Framlington?'

'No folly, no game, sir. I loved your daughter from the

commencement of my courtship. I know my only means comes from Mary, but I will look after her, love her and cherish her. I understand why you do not approve of me, but I promise she will be happy.'

'You made my daughter miserable in London.' Marlow's cold, assessing gaze bore into Drew.

Drew swallowed back his shame. 'I felt humiliated before her, by my family. I did not think she would want a man like me.'

'But she does, it would seem.'

'Yes, sir, Mary does want me, and I thank God for it.'

Marlow's arms unfolded. 'I have always judged people by their actions. Actions speak far louder than words. Your actions towards your sister speak of what is underneath your anger...'

'Sir?'

'You have not treated my daughter well to date. But Mary told me you have sworn to hold your temper and stop these antagonistic outbursts. This conversation implies you mean that. I hope to see the actions that prove it in the future too.'

'You must understand my family's circumstances—'

'I know it. Mary has told me everything.'

Drew fell silent. Unsure what to say.

'The slate is wiped clean. You have my consent. Or rather, you have my endorsement,' he said. Drew swallowed as Marlow walked towards him. He gripped Drew's shoulder, as a father might. 'Do not let me down, son. Now may we go to dinner? I am hungry.'

Son? Emotion wrenched in Drew's chest, an odd pain.

He shook his head. 'Lord Marlow—'

'Edward, at least, or Father if you wish, as you have none of your own.'

'Thank you.'

Marlow smiled slightly. 'You are welcome. Now do you see how things could have been, if you had done them right?'

Drew took a breath; he was on unsteady ground. 'I am sorry I did not.'

Marlow's smile twisted, wryly. 'Well, Mary has forgiven you. So, I forgive you. I am man enough for that. But remember, it is on a provision, no more foolishness.'

When they left the room, Drew discovered Mary waiting in the hall.

One hand wrapped around Drew's upper arm, and the other hand pressed there too as they walked towards the formal drawing room. He remembered her doing the same when they ran away. Cupid's arrow struck him firmly through the heart, the shaft quivering.

Mary talked to her father as they entered the room.

Bless her. She understood his confusion and was giving him time to adjust. *She always understood.* The conversation in the drawing room fell silent. Mary's hand released Drew's arm.

He could not move, his body became so tense.

She held his hand instead.

Drew saw Richard. Her uncle lifted his hands and clapped, the motion and the sound spread about the people in the room, until everyone was applauding.

When the applause ceased, Andrew tensed even more as her uncles and some older cousins approached him.

'I admire your courage.'

'Good work.'

'Congratulations.'

Mary released his hand, because they all wanted to shake it.

'I am proud to know you.'

'Well done.'

Andrew accepted their comments with nods and brief nervous smiles as he was told not to bother with titles and pomp.

His hand searched for Mary's.

She took it.

His fingers closed about hers and clung on.

* * *

Andrew's heartbeat pulsed in the hand that held hers, the pace quicker than it had been when they stood on the stairs. He was fighting the bewilderment he felt among her family.

Her brother Robbie was the next to approach. She had longed to introduce them.

'Lord Framlington, I am pleased to meet you. I should imagine life was pretty grim in that prison cell?' he said, with the eagerness of an adolescent.

'Robbie,' Mary chided. 'I have not even introduced you. Andrew, this is the eldest of my younger brothers, Robbie.'

'You did not say I am your favourite brother, as she is my favourite sister.' Robbie grinned broadly as he held out a hand to shake Andrew's.

Andrew released her hand and accepted his. 'Hello, favourite brother. It *was* extremely miserable in prison, it is not a place I would recommend.'

She knew from the glint in Andrew's eyes that he liked Robbie instantly, but Robbie was such an easy-going, happy person, no one could feel uncomfortable around him.

'My brother, Harry, and me, are notorious at college now, thanks to you. Everyone wishes to know us because our sister ran away with a scoundrel.'

'Robbie!'

'The lad is not offending me, Mary.' Andrew smiled. 'I am glad I brought you notoriety. Where is your brother?'

'With the children.' Robbie glanced at Mary. 'He got into trouble at college for a prank so Papa would not let him come down.'

Mary rolled her eyes. 'Typical Harry.'

Andrew's fingers touched her arm. 'Where is Caro?'

'Seated in the corner by the window. You may quiz Andrew later, Robbie.'

Robbie grinned. 'Indeed.' He turned away, understanding the dismissal.

Mary saw that Caroline was watching them. She had not been left alone, Mary's mother sat beside her, because, like Andrew, Caroline struggled to cope with this crowd of people. Everyone had tried to include her, but she did not want to be included, she preferred to be left alone.

As Andrew crossed the room, his hand holding hers again, members of her family continually delayed them, stopping Andrew to welcome and congratulate him. His hold on her hand became tenser. It was becoming too much.

When they reached Caroline, she smiled at him and Andrew let go of Mary and sank down on his haunches. 'How are you?'

Tears trailed down Caroline's cheeks as she leaned forward and enveloped him in her arms. They progressed the conversation in whispers spoken to each other's ears.

Mary had always been close to Robbie, but she could see the closeness between Andrew and Caroline ran deeper; it was born of mutual suffering, not just a blood connection.

Something touched Mary's arm. She glanced back. Her father held out his handkerchief.

She took it. Then touched Caroline's shoulder and offered the handkerchief to her.

'Thank you.' Caroline sniffed back tears as she accepted it, glancing at Mary's father for only an instant.

'All will be well, now,' Andrew said to Caroline then stood and looked at her father. 'I thought you were hungry, are we not going to eat?'

Her father chuckled, and raised a hand, which clearly told someone in the room they were ready as a moment later the dinner gong rang.

Andrew smiled apologetically at Mary, as he offered his arm to Caroline. But it had to be so.

Mary's father offered his arm to Mary. They let Andrew lead Caroline into the dining room ahead of them. 'I like him, now,' her father said quietly. 'But he is still on trial. Had he said he loved you in the beginning, instead of walking away with that cheque less than an hour after you were wed, with a cocky grin on his face, I might already trust him completely. But I have rarely wished to kill a man as much as that.'

'He will not let me down, Papa. I know he won't.'

Her father withdrew a chair for her to sit, rather than leaving the task to a footman. Then walked further along the table to sit beside her mother.

As Mary ate, raucous conversation, laughter and deeper discussions passed across the table, while Andrew and Caroline spoke exclusively to each other in low tones.

41

When Kate rose and led the women from the room, to leave the men at the table, Mary heard Caroline tell Andrew she was going to her room.

'Then I will leave the table and walk up with you,' he answered. He smiled at Mary. 'I will meet you in the drawing room.'

She nodded.

The men were still at the dinner table when Andrew came down, and the women were listening to Mary's cousin Margaret playing the pianoforte. He looked about, unsure what to do. Mary stood and went to him, and in the same moment the men came back, drifting in in groups.

'Let us dance!' Mary's cousin Eleanor called, clapping her hands to silence the room. Some of the men moved furniture aside to make space.

'I am only participating if we are dancing waltzes!' Mary's father shouted at Eleanor.

'And he will then only dance with Mama,' Mary whispered to Andrew. 'Will you dance with me? We have never danced a waltz.'

He smiled. 'Yes. If that is what you want.'

He had promised her tolerance; she knew this was that. 'I will sit it out if you prefer.'

His smile twisted and he leaned to her ear. 'I am sorry if I seemed reluctant, it is just all evening I have felt your family watching. I do not like to be the entertainment. At least if they are dancing, they will have another occupation.'

'Look at me. Do not think of them.'

Margaret played a slow waltz. There were too many couples in the room, and too much furniture, for them to dance boldly.

'Happy?' Andrew asked, as he spun her over-exuberantly.

'Now you are here, yes. And *only* when you are here.'

His smile tilted sideways and he leaned to her ear. 'Your father called me son.'

'Then he approves of you.'

'He approves if I am good for you. I am being good.'

'You were always good for me, even when you were very bad.'

A chuckle rumbled in his throat. 'Do I have permission to be bad sometimes then?'

'As if you have ever awaited permission.'

She was pulled flush against him in response, her thighs moving against his, as her breasts crushed against his chest.

She would have backed away and told him off, but every couple in the room danced closer than they would in a ballroom among the rest of the *ton*.

It was enticing. She understood when it was danced like this why some matrons hated the dance.

When Margaret ended the piece of music, as they waited for the next tune, Mary looked into wide onyx pupils with glimmering gold edges and knew what he was thinking.

As Margaret began another tune, his head bent and his teeth

nipped her neck just below her ear, so it might look as though he had whispered.

She nearly fell, but he held her, a note of humour in his throat.

'You are being wicked.'

'You said you like me bad.' He missed a step, and she tripped, only to be caught in his arms. 'You muddle me up, Mary.'

He did it again and made her laugh out loud. It was what he had intended. But he could not have intended that they bump into her father and mother.

'Sorry, Papa, Mama. Andrew is making mistakes to make me laugh.'

Her father lifted an eyebrow, but he smiled before dancing on.

Andrew leaned to her ear. 'Have you told your parents about the child? Your father said nothing to me.'

'No.'

'Your uncle knows. I told him in town. So, we had best tell your parents before they hear it from him.'

When Margaret played the last notes, Andrew broke their embrace, took a firm hold of Mary's hand and walked the few steps to where her father and mother stood. 'Sir?'

'My name is Edward.' Her father smiled.

'Edward, then, sir, we would like a word if we may?'

'What is it?' Mary's mother asked.

'My lady, I—'

'It is Ellen, Andrew, until you are able to think of me as a mother.'

Andrew took a breath to get the words out. 'Mary is with child. She has just informed me that you did not yet know and I wanted to tell you.' His fingers threaded in between Mary's while he spoke.

For a moment they were silent. Mary's teeth pressed into her lower lip. Then her father reached out to shake Andrew's hand, moisture glinting in his eyes.

Her mother's eyes swam as she reached to embrace Mary. 'I am happy for you, I have been so worried...'

'Are you pleased, Andrew?' her father said.

'Sir, I mean,' Andrew sighed, 'Edward, yes, very much, and John is selling me a property adjoining his. We will live near here so Mary will have her brother close—'

'I know about the property. John does talk to me.' Mary's father patted Andrew's shoulder, then he turned to the room and raised a hand. 'A moment! Let us have your attention! My son-in-law has some news!'

Margaret's fingers stilled on the keys of the pianoforte and couples swung to a halt.

Andrew swallowed, as though his throat were dry. 'Mary is with child!'

More handshaking and good wishes followed.

'If you desire more waltzes, then,' Margaret's husband shouted, 'someone else shall have to play. I want to dance with my wife!'

Laughter rippled across the room.

Eleanor swapped places with Margaret, and Eleanor ignored the size of the room and the number of couples and played a raucous tune, which had everyone bumping into each other and laughing.

After three dances, Andrew leant and whispered in her ear, 'I have had my fill of playing happy families, Mary, darling. Do you mind if we go outside?'

'Of course not.'

They escaped through a French door that stood ajar to cool the room. The evening air outside was tepid but not cold, and a full moon hung in the sky illuminating everything.

She walked backwards towards the terrace's balustrade as he withdrew a cigar and a match from his coat pocket.

'The night is lovely, the stars are beautiful.'

'You are lovelier,' he answered.

She leaned her bottom against the balustrade. 'Idle flattery will earn you nothing.'

'So you said when I sent you that damn poetry.' He struck the match on the stone, and lifted the flame to the cigar's tip, illuminating his face. She had quite liked him with his beard earlier, his handsomeness was always borne of rugged masculinity.

He shook the flame out and tossed the match away. 'Poor Peter put so much effort into those words. They were mostly his. If you would ever like prose, tell me and I will call on Peter. I have asked him to be godfather, by the way. I hope you do not mind.'

He rested his buttocks on the balustrade, one hand on the stone, the other holding his cigar.

'I do not mind.' In the moonlight, beneath the stars, their story felt a little like a fairy tale, only she had not fallen for a prince. If it was a fairy tale, it was beauty and the beast.

'Are you surviving?' she asked him.

'Your family?' A low, deep, mocking sound slipped from his throat. 'Yes, they are a little overpowering when one is not used to them. Though, I surprise myself at times, I think I am coping admirably. I surprised myself when I wrote out those letters too. I thought I could not write sweet nothings, but when I sat down and rewrote what they scribbled half drunk, the emotions flowed into my words.'

She frowned. 'Your words? Your friends wrote them.'

'The last paragraph of the second letter was my own, and the letters thereafter.' He gave her a self-deprecating smile.

'"*My Mary, you are, you know, mine. You always will be,*"' she quoted.

His lips twitched, a smile hovering but not forming.

"'*You and I are meant to be one, half to become whole. Put us together, make us one, a single being. I want you,*'" she progressed as he sucked on the cigar and blew the smoke upwards, away from her.

Mary's heart thumped hard against her ribs. "'*You and I are meant to be one, hand and glove, half and whole. Put us together, darling, make us one, a single being...*" Were they your words?'

A frown creased the skin of his forehead. 'Yes, probably, I do not remember them in that much detail. But I sat down that morning and they came spilling out of me. I did not want to lose you.'

She had read those words again and again in the last few days. Even though she had believed they were not his, she had clung on to the sentiment in them. "'*I cannot say I love you, not yet, I do not even know what on earth love is, but I do know that I cannot sleep for thinking of you or avoid dreaming of you. I think of you and I lose my breath. I see you and my heart begins to pound. I hear you and my spirit wants to sing. I am yours, Mary. Be mine...*

"'*Think of the possibilities. If this is love? If this is our only chance? If we are meant to be, would you throw that away? Throw me away?*'"

He smiled his roguish grin and shook his head. 'You memorised those letters. No wonder you were so hurt when you found out they were not written by me.'

'I did not memorise that other nonsense, but those words... They were yours?'

He sucked on his cigar again, eyeing her with amusement. 'Yes.'

'It was only those words that made me believe you.' Tears misted her gaze.

'I wanted it to be like this,' he said.

'Like this?' She straightened up and turned towards him. 'I am sure you did not imagine us here, with my family a few feet away.'

'No.' He laughed. 'I did not imagine them. But you loving me, as I loved you, that is what I longed for.'

'That you have always had,' she answered.

He extinguished his cigar and threw the stub into the flowerbeds. 'Let us be naughty and abscond. I do not want to go back in there. I have a better idea than waltzes.'

She glanced at the open French door.

'Come on, my rebel. They know you are safe.'

Her loyalty belonged to him first, and she did not want to bridle her wild, restless stallion tonight when he had only just earned his freedom again.

'Come on.' He grasped her hand. He must have seen the decision in her eyes.

They ran down the steps and across the lawn.

'Where are we going?'

'To the lake!'

He pulled her on.

With her free hand, she lifted her evening dress above her knees and ran as she had done earlier. When they ran from the formal garden into the meadow, the long grass swiped at her legs, and their footsteps flooded the night air with the scents from the heads of clover.

She was breathing hard when they reached the water.

The lake was absolutely still, reflecting the night sky and the full moon.

Andrew slowed to a walk, but led her further around the lake, not stopping until the house was out of sight.

'Here.' He stripped off his evening coat and lay it down. Then released the buttons of his waistcoat.

'What are you doing?' she asked.

'We are going for a swim, sweetheart.'

'Andrew, I am in an evening gown.'

'Did I say we were swimming in our clothes? Undress.'

'What if someone comes?'

'We will make lots of noise and they will hear us and leave us in privacy.'

'They will think...'

'That we are a newly married couple enjoying ourselves.' He dropped his waistcoat on the grass.

'Andrew—'

'Mary. We are married, no one will judge.' His fingers pulled the knot of his cravat loose. 'If you say no, you will always wish you had said, yes. Do not lack courage.' His cravat slid from around his neck. 'Let me undo your dress for you.'

Giving in to his urging, she turned her back.

He released one button, then the next, his fingers brushing against bare skin. 'You are not wearing stays, or a chemise.'

'The satin falls better with nothing beneath, underwear spoils the silhouette of this dress, and now I am married I may be daring and wear what I like.'

'See, I said you were a rebel. You should have told me earlier you wore no underwear beneath, I would not have bothered dancing,' he joked as his fingers released the rest of the buttons. When they were loose, his hands slipped about her, beneath the satin, and cupped her breasts. His lips brushed kisses across her neck as his palms squeezed.

When she had met him in the dark glasshouse, long ago, hiding from her family, his caresses had been dangerous and desperate. Now they felt like home; a place she wished to be.

'This has just become my favourite dress,' he said as his fingers slid it off her shoulders and in one fall, the dress slithered to the ground, leaving her wearing an odd combination of gloves, stockings and shoes.

The night air felt cooler here, by the lake.

While she finished undressing, he picked up her dress, folded it carefully and lay it on his coat.

'My hair...' It was ornately styled, held in place with many small pearl-headed pins.

'I shall take out the pins, and you can plait it.'

'I cannot swim,' she confessed.

'I will hold you up,' he said as he pulled off his shirt. He threw that on the ground, kicked off his shoes and released the buttons at the waist of his trousers. 'You do not realise how beautiful you are, even now, do you? You are head to toe perfect. Flawless.' He stripped off his trousers, underwear and stockings in one swift movement, and left them in a small heap. 'Your skin is luminous in the moonlight.' He smiled. 'It draws my eyes to that mound of dark hair at your woman-hood, and it pleases me that you are not trying to cover yourself.'

When she turned her back to him, so he could begin removing pins, one cheek of her bottom brushed his hip. Desire pulsed, but she ignored the urge to lie down with him.

She shivered in the breeze sweeping up from the lake. Her arms crossed over her breasts, rubbing her upper arms. 'We should have fetched a blanket before coming out here.'

He placed the cupped hand full of pearl-headed pins into a pocket of his coat.

She released the clasp of her pearl necklace and handed it to him.

As he slipped the necklace into another pocket, her fingers wove her long dark hair into a braid.

'I shall dive in from that branch,' he said. 'Then you can jump in after me and I will catch you.'

She was not convinced she could do it.

He pulled her close and kissed her briefly, before leading her to the willow tree that had a thick branch stretching out over the water.

When he dived, Andrew slipped into the shining jet-black water like an arrow, fracturing its surface and leaving only a ring of ripples as he disappeared beneath. A moment later, he reappeared a few yards from the bank, shaking the water from his hair. That devil-may-care grin on his lips.

'Jump in!' he called. 'Be brave, darling! I will catch you!'

The dark water shimmered with the reflected light of the moon and stars.

She had watched her brothers swimming with her father but she had never swum.

'Come on!'

If she was to trust him now, then she should trust him in everything.

She walked along the branch he had dived from, holding the smaller branches above her head. Then before she could renege, she jumped in, feet first. The water consumed her in a cold grip and her feet kicked at a tangle of weeds. Her arms flailed, her heart pounding.

Then a solid band caught about her middle, below her breasts, and pulled her to the surface.

'Relax, I have you.'

She rested her body back against his chest as he floated up beneath her, his legs kicking at the water.

'Don't let me go.'

'I would not, darling. I do not want to lose you. Now, I will hold your hands, but I want you to lie flat on your back, floating, with your arms and legs wide as though you were lying on a bed.

Let every muscle slacken, as if you were falling asleep on a bed of water.'

Mary looked up at the stars, and felt her body rise as his hold slipped to her hands. Her feet bobbed up on the water, and it lapped at her breasts that her pregnancy had increased. Her stomach touched the surface too, and the sway of the water was a gentle caress on her naked skin.

'There, stay just so. I will let you go and you will not sink if you stay relaxed. I shall be here, just behind you.'

Her heart thumped, as he released her hands, and her bottom sank a little, but she did float. For a moment it was wonderful as she stared at the stars and felt like she was in the heavens with them. But then her feet started sinking, and she forgot how to be weightless. He grabbed her arm and stopped her sinking further.

'Put your arms about my neck and I will swim for us.'

She kicked clumsily at the water, holding his shoulders, riding on his back, his body sleek and strong beneath her while he swam, his legs and arms moving like a frog's legs.

The moonlight glittered on the ripples they created.

The park seemed even more beautiful in the darkness. It felt like a secret beauty.

He turned suddenly, his body floating up beneath hers.

'Do you want to try and swim?'

'No.'

'Wrong answer, darling. Of course you do. Do not be afraid, I will hold your hands, put your legs out straight and kick your feet.'

She did as he bid her; he held her hands and swam backwards while she swam forwards, her feet splashing at the surface.

'If you keep your feet beneath the surface, it will propel you better.'

She did as he said.

'I shall let go of your hands, then you must slide your hands backwards, pushing the water out of your way, bring your hands forwards and do the same again.'

Panic caught in her throat as he let her go, but she did as he said, and her body moved without sinking. He swam backwards in front of her, speaking words of encouragement.

'You said you could not swim, but you can, see.'

'You said my family would not like you, but they do, see.'

'Do not make me laugh, I will drown, and then where will you be? There is a river near our property, we can swim often when we live there. Do you not agree it is much better than waltzing?'

'Yes.' Her legs kicked hard, as her arms pushed the water back and circled around to do it again.

'Are you ready to get out? I think this is enough for your first lesson.'

'How will we get out?' There were no shallow places along the bank.

'The boating jetty. Hold my shoulders again and we will swim there.'

'The boating jetty? How did you know about that? Did you plan this?'

He smiled his roguish smile. 'I admit I noted the places where the lake cannot be seen from the front of the house after John said they watched us when we sat down here. Then while you rested in the afternoons, I had time to explore the places to get in and out of the water. But the opportunity to indulge never came until now.'

'You are wicked.'

'And you love me for it.'

'Yes, I do.'

The jetty reached out about seven yards from the shore.

'You climb out first, press your palms down on the wood and I will push you up.' He pushed on one cheek of her bottom, which had her tumbling onto the jetty in giggles.

His palms pressed on the wood, the muscles bunching in his arms as he rose from the water, the moonlight glistening on his damp skin and hair, highlighting the ridges and hollows of his muscular architecture.

I am a lucky woman.

They walked along the jetty and back about the lake holding hands. She did not care she was naked, because she knew what would come now, and she ached for it to happen. But he waited until they reached the willow tree before he kissed her; his palm embracing her nape and the pressure of his lips warm and strong. She opened her mouth, leading the touch of their tongues. His erection pressed against her stomach and his other hand cupped her buttock, while her hands trailed over his damp skin.

'I wanted to be patient and slow, Mary, but I cannot.' His lips lifted to a smile against her lips. 'I love you too much. I am too eager with you.'

His hands wrapped about her upper thighs, firm and strong, his fingertips pressing into skin and muscle as he lifted her legs to his hips. He dropped to his knees, leaned her back and lay her down, the water on her skin probably staining the silk lining of the evening coat he put down for them earlier. He held her so carefully, it was as though he thought if he was too rough, she might break. Then he slid into her, pressing deep into her soul as well as her body.

'I love you,' he said as he withdrew to his tip and pushed back in, beginning a slow firm rhythm. He pressed kisses across her face, on her cheek, her eyelids, enthralling every inch of her.

'Andrew!' She called out his name as the inner sensations spun, whipping up into a whirlpool.

His movements became swifter and stronger. Pain and pleasure fought.

His movement changed to a shallow pulse that made her want to scream for his depth. Then his hands, fingers splayed, drew her thighs wider apart and his strokes became ruthless with unsatiable hunger.

'Mary.' He growled her name. 'I want you undone. Have no restraint!'

A whirlpool raced inside her. The sensations spinning through her nerves. The soles of her bare feet pressed into the backs of his thighs as her fingertips clung to his shoulders, and her breasts rocked with his heavy thrusts.

Then... She slipped across the edge and fell. Crying out, with a long animalistic sound she would not have thought could come from her throat.

'You are everything I have ever wanted,' he said as his pelvis struck hers with a new force. His weight pressing down on her and into her repeatedly.

Her thighs trembled as she tried to push back against him, until she fell to her little death again.

He held still, his release pulsing inside her body as his head dropped, hanging down so that his damp hair brushed her cheek.

When his head lifted, he smiled. She smiled too.

'You beautiful woman. You make me feel like a king.' He withdrew and rolled onto his back.

She laid against his side, one arm and leg slipping across his body as her palm settled on his chest.

They laid in silence then. She could hear the music from the house. Someone must have opened all the French doors for the music to travel so far.

'I wish we could sleep here, but someone will find us eventually. We must dress and go back.'

'I am still wet, the water will ruin my dress.'

'Then wear my shirt. We can go in via the servants' hall.' He got up.

'I would horrify the servants if I walked in in your shirt. They will be tidying up after dinner and preparing for the morning, their hall will be full at this hour.'

He held out his hand to help her up. 'Then go in through the front door and hope no one is in the hall. The choice is yours, sweetheart, ruin your dress or take the risk.'

She accepted his hand and he pulled her to her feet.

He picked up his trousers. 'I will add that as I now love that dress, I vote for the latter option.' His smile was wry.

She pouted, and made a face at him, that made him laugh. 'You did not plan this as well as you thought.' She huffed, then picked up his shirt. It fell to her mid-thigh, covering very little.

'In the future, I shall include you in my planning.' He gathered up the rest of their clothes, careful not to let her hair pins or necklace slip from the pockets of his coat. He in just his trousers, and she in just his shirt, with their other clothes under his arm, she held his hand and they walked towards the house, the white cotton of his shirt catching the moonlight and making her stand out in the dark meadow.

She hoped everyone was still at the back of the house, and no one was looking out from the front windows.

When they reached the gravel drive, she stepped tentatively on to it.

'Wait.' Drew slipped on his shoes. 'Here, take these.' He passed her the pile of clothing, then swung her up into his arms so swiftly she squealed.

'If you are trying not to be seen, shouting is not the way to go about it, Mary, darling.'

When they reached the smooth stone steps of the portico, he let her feet fall, took their clothes back and held her hand again.

She turned the door handle slowly and quietly, hoping not to alert a footman. There was no one inside, and the noise from the drawing room was loud, meaning they were unlikely to be heard. She ran across the cold marble floor, smiling at their scandalous behaviour, and hurried upstairs with Andrew ahead of her. They encountered no one.

Within her rooms, as soon as she had shut the door, Andrew pressed her back against it, their clothes dropping on the floor.

Once he had asked her if she thought she had stepped from her heaven into his hell. No, this was her heaven.

42

A footman walked quickly into the family dining room, interrupting breakfast. 'A carriage is approaching, Your Grace.'

'How far away?'

Drew looked towards the windows, as though he would be able to see.

'Five minutes, perhaps.'

Would Kilbride be fool enough to come here? Drew stood.

John glanced at him, his expression saying he had the same thought.

Caro had not come downstairs. She was eating in her rooms. At least if it was Kilbride she would be nowhere near and he could not abuse her in any way.

Drew walked from the room. The feet of Mary's chair scraped on the parquet floor as she rose to follow him.

Other members of her family followed too.

Drew ignored his audience and walked through the hall. A footman hurried forward and opened the front door. Drew walked outside. If this was Kilbride, he would face him head on.

By the time he walked down the front steps, John had caught up and walked beside him. Mary caught him up too, and her hand slipped into his.

As the carriage came into view, he was surrounded by all the men of her family.

'It is Lord Brooke!' Drew shouted. The shield emblazoned on the side was that of his friend's.

The men about him drifted away.

He let go of Mary's hand as the carriage driver pulled the reins to halt the horses. John's grooms rushed forward, and one man opened the door before Drew could reach it.

Peter stepped down, grinning broadly. 'Good day, my friend. I told you I would call on you.'

Harry stepped from the carriage behind him, then Mark behind him.

Drew embraced them all, one at a time, realising he had always known love. He loved these men. He also knew them well enough that he saw through their tactics, they had arrived en masse to make it harder for John to turn any of them away.

But when Drew glanced at John, he merely smiled, and nodded at Peter in a way that said, *hello*. To the others he said, 'Welcome. There is breakfast on the table if you are hungry.'

The pride of Pembroke lions had turned away, but Mary hovered.

'Would you mind if I walk through the park alone with them, sweetheart?'

She smiled and nodded her acceptance. Her father offered his arm to her.

Drew was a fool to have fought her family. They were never against him, just for Mary. He and her father had always been on the same side really.

Brooke held Drew's shoulder. 'Oh, ye of little faith, did I not say all would be well? The rest of the world shuns you and your wife's family takes the wolf into the fold.'

'He was only ever a lamb really.' Harry laughed.

'I am still working on my prose to win Miss Smithfield,' Peter said.

'Oh, about your prose...' Drew felt a smug smile pull up his lips. 'Mary never liked it. It was no help at all. It was the words I added that she liked.'

'Dammit, then I have no chance!' Peter protested, smiling. 'You shall have to write my love letters, that is all.'

'I think Mary would be better at it, you may ask her.'

Drew looked at Mark and Harry. 'Has Peter told you? Mary is expecting a child.'

'No, I saved that thunder for the proud papa.'

Mark and Harry could not hide their shock.

'My God.'

'Good grief, I will be an uncle.'

Yes, these men were his family. His surrogate brothers. He wished them all to be in his child's life.

When Drew saw Mary striding out in their direction, they had been walking and talking for a long while. 'Would you like to come into the house to take tea?' Mary called when she was within hearing distance.

His friends declined. They were not a home and hearth bunch. It made Drew look through a window into his old life, when he would have said the same about himself.

He preferred his new one, and he would make the most of every day of it.

Mary stayed with them until they said farewell. They all kissed her cheek, and she invited them to visit again, making sure they knew they were welcome here. Drew held Mary's waist as they waved his friends off.

This was his home – she was his home. A woman who loved him with her whole heart, and a woman he loved with the whole of his. His Mary.

EPILOGUE

Drew leaned back against the broad trunk of the old oak, cradling little George in his arms, and crooning to the child. He had stolen his son from the nursery maid while Mary slept. George was already two months old and summer was setting in again. Spring's blossoms had turned to green leaves to shade George from the sunshine which was nourishing the crops Drew had helped to plant in the fields.

His son's fingers wrapped about Drew's thumb.

Every time he looked into the boy's eyes his heart melted. He adored his son. He had hated naming him Framlington, yet that was the name he had and thus it was his son's. But a name was not the thing that made a man.

He could tell George had strength of will and purpose, even now. It was in his grip of Drew's thumb. He had been determined to come out when he wished to, not waiting for a midwife, a doctor, or even his aunt to arrive. Drew was the one who caught his son, when George slithered from Mary's body.

Ever since that moment, George had Drew wrapped around

his little finger. The only hardship was to leave the child in his cradle.

George gurgled, kicking a single leg free of his loose blanket; a strong healthy leg. The boy was getting fractious, hungry for a feed, the one thing his son could not get from his father. But everything else, everything else, he could.

Drew rose and walked across the front lawn to the house. Caro was sitting outside on a bench. She doted on his son too, but he knew she also remembered the children she had lost.

He touched her shoulder. 'Would you like to hold George briefly? He is due a feed and getting fractious but it will do him no harm to wait a moment, before I take him to Mary?'

'No. He wants his mother and his milk.' She smiled, but it did not reach her eyes. 'Go on. I am happy here.'

'Very well.' He smiled too, then walked on.

He had tried to cheer her, but she refused to take part in social engagements and she would hide in her rooms when people called. It was only when he and Mary were there that she would occasionally dine with them, and sit around the house reading or sewing, or come into the garden to cut flowers or gather seeds. She may be physically free of Kilbride, but she was still imprisoned by him. At least her divorce would complete soon.

When he entered the front hall, Mary stood with her hand on the newel post of the dark oak staircase, her eyes looking glassy from sleep. She looked even more beautiful, womanlier, with her breasts swollen with milk.

She held out her hands to take George. 'I was just coming to fetch him.'

'I will come upstairs with you.'

* * *

Andrew's eyes glowed like warm honey, as he watched her feed George.

'Where were you?' she asked.

'Sitting beneath the trees, enjoying the day. He likes the leaves swaying above his head.'

She glanced down at George, whose eyes were shut while he sucked. His little hand rested on her breast.

'When Papa came to see George, he said you are an excellent father.'

He laughed. 'I recall being called many things by your father a year ago, and excellent was not among them. But if I am, it is because I adore you both.'

'That was before Papa knew you. You know he and Mama love you now.'

His eyes glittered with amusement, devil-may-care thoughts shining in them. Fatherhood and marriage had not made him any less of a rogue. When the family met at John's, he was always whipping the children up into a riot with boisterous games. For a man who had shied away from her family, he was now a pivotal part. Mary only wished that Caro would join in and find happiness too.

A smile twisted Andrew's lips. 'I think the next time I see Edward, I shall call him Papa, and see how he reacts.'

'He will love that.'

* * *

MORE FROM JANE LARK

Another book from Jane Lark, *The Secret Love of a Gentleman*, is available to order now here:

https://mybook.to/SecretLoveBackAd

AUTHOR NOTE

The inspiration for this story came to me when I read the letters of Lady Caroline Lamb, whose family history was thickly woven with that of Harriette Wilson, the Regency courtesan whose memoirs inspired the Marlow family series.

If you would like to discover some of the real stories that inspired elements of this fictional tale, then you will find them on my blog http://janelark.blog/.

Drew and Mary will be back to play a large part in the next Marlow Secrets story, *The Secret Love of a Gentleman*, and in that story Lady Kilbride, Caro, will discover her well-deserved happy ever after too...

ABOUT THE AUTHOR

Jane Lark is a writer of compelling, passionate and emotionally charged fiction filled with diverse characters. She is an international bestselling author of both historical fiction and psychological thrillers, and a finalist in British Fiction Industry awards.

Sign up to Jane Lark's mailing list for news, competitions and updates on future books.

Visit Jane's website: www.janelark.co.uk

Follow Jane on social media here:

X x.com/JaneLark

facebook.com/Janelarkauthor

instagram.com/jane.lark

youtube.com/@janelark3537

BB bookbub.com/authors/jane-lark

ALSO BY JANE LARK

The Great Western Railway Girls Series

The Great Western Railway Girls

The Marlow Family Secrets Series

The Dangerous Love of a Rogue

The Seductive Love of a Lady

The Secret Love of a Gentleman

The Reckless Love of an Heir

You're cordially invited to

The Scandal Sheet

The home of swoon-worthy
historical romance from the
Regency to the Victorian era!

Warning: may contain spice

Sign up to the newsletter

https://bit.ly/thescandalsheet

Boldwood

Boldwood Books is an award-winning fiction publishing company seeking out the best stories from around the world.

Find out more at www.boldwoodbooks.com

Join our reader community for brilliant books, competitions and offers!

Follow us
@BoldwoodBooks
@TheBoldBookClub

Sign up to our weekly
deals newsletter

https://bit.ly/BoldwoodBNewsletter

Printed in Dunstable, United Kingdom

Printed in Dunstable, United Kingdom